Forty South
Short Story
Anthology 2022

THE ELEVEN BEST ENTRIES FROM THE
TASMANIAN WRITERS' PRIZE 2022

Selected by

ANNIE WARBURTON   MEG BIGNELL   RAYNE ALLINSON

40

Editor: Chris Champion
Layout and design: Forty South Publishing Pty Ltd

Publisher: Forty South Publishing Pty Ltd
Hobart, Tasmania
fortysouth.com.au

Printer: IngramSpark

Cover: Summer rain on the Ray Range by Peter Marmion

Contents

40

FORTY SOUTH PUBLISHING

The Tasmanian Writers' Prize

The Tasmanian Writers' Prize began in 2009 and, in order to promote and support writers, each year Forty South has published the winning story in *FortySouth* and produced an annual anthology of the best entries. Since 2014 the competition has been themed on the concept of 'island' and is open to residents of Australia and New Zealand.

WINNERS OF THE TASMANIAN WRITERS' PRIZE

2009 (2010 anthology)	John Hale (TAS)	Ferry
2010 (2011 anthology)	Leigh Swinbourne (TAS)	Away
2011 (2012 anthology)	Kate Esser (TAS)	Crossing water
2013	Debi Hamilton (VIC)	Mud flats
2014	Polly Whittington (TAS)	The chimney pot
2015	Rachel Leary (VIC)	A concrete Aborigine
2016	Craig Cormick (ACT)	No man is an island
2017	Jennifer Porter (VIC)	The Reverend
2018	Melissa Manning (VIC)	Boy
2019	Greg Burgess (TAS)	Pilgrims
2020	Andrea McMahon (TAS)	Damselfly
2021	RI Quin (QLD)	Saving Daniel
2022	Christine Betts (NSW)	How I got this tattoo

To order copies of the anthologies or to view other
Forty South Publishing titles visit:
fortysouth.com.au and go to our Forty South Bookshop
Email: accounts@fortysouth.com.au
Post: PO Box 168 Lindisfarne TAS 7015

The judges

ANNIE WARBURTON is a lawyer turned broadcaster and writer. She joined the ABC after leaving the Australian Legal Aid Office in Darwin in 1983. She has worked mostly in local radio and TV but has written, presented and produced features for ABC current affairs and Radio National. Warburton moved to her ancestral Tasmania in 1990. She has served on the committee of Tasmania's literary magazine, Island, and was Tasmanian contributor to SCOSE – the Standing Committee On Spoken English. Since retiring from the ABC, she has set up her own website where she publishes reviews, travel writing and social commentary. She has been a presenter and interviewer with the Tamar Valley Writers Festival in recent years, and is currently writing for the independent regional newspaper *The New Norfolk and Derwent Valley News*.

MEG BIGNELL began her writing career as a trainee copywriter with Win Television Tasmania. She went on to work as a commercial and corporate producer, presenter and director for regional television and later as a medical researcher, writer and on-set advisor for the Network Seven drama *All Saints*. She continues to write for corporate clients, for stage and film and is the author of three novels – *The Sparkle Pages* (2019), *Welcome to Nowhere River* (2021) and *The Angry Women's Choir* (2022) – all published by Penguin Random House.

RAYNE ALLINSON is a writer and teacher with a PhD in History from the University of Oxford. She is the author of *A Monarchy of Letters: Royal correspondence and English diplomacy in the reign of Elizabeth I* (2012). She has worked and travelled in many parts of the northern hemisphere, and is now based in southern Tasmania and working as Assistant Publisher at Forty South Publishing. She is also a regular contributor to *Forty South Tasmania* and runs the Reading Group at Fullers Bookshop.

Judges' comments

In the words of Irish Booker-prize-winning author, Roddy Doyle, "When you grow up on an island, what matters is how you stand to the sea." Because of their liminality, islands can represent many contrary things. Isolation and connection. Permanence and change. They might be easily charted on a map, but something about them remains hidden, mysterious, unreachable. "Islands are metaphors of the heart", Jeannette Winterson writes, "no matter what poet says otherwise."

This year we received eighty-five stories from all around Australia and New Zealand, and each took their own unique stance on the theme of "islands". We had stories on emergency rescues, imagined flights from post-apocalyptic landscapes, surreal visions of death (or birth?) by water, romance gone wrong at sea, dangerous journeys into deep waters, tender evocations of literary love affairs, haunting glimpses of ghostly forms, disturbing portraits of misogynistic minds, the isolating effects of old age, and new beginnings summoned from the relentless pulse of the tide.

We were drawn to stories with vivid characters and startling situations, stories that made us laugh, or think, or feel. We also sought out flawless spelling, grammar, and punctuation, which are the hallmarks of good craftsmanship.

Our winning story, "How I got this tattoo", did all these things and left us eager for more. Written in a lucid, conversational style, it captures a moment of shared understanding between women, and shows (with disarming humour) how flashes of insight can burst forth in the most unlikely circumstances.

Our judges Annie Warburton, Meg Bignell, and Rayne Allinson would like to thank all the entrants to the Tasmanian Writers' Prize 2022, and offer congratulations to our winner and 10 finalists.

"Place" is central to CHRISTINE BETTS' work. Christine left her heart in Paris years ago and her first two novels and a collection of short stories are all set in France. Current works in progress are set in California, England, and, because we've all mostly been grounded over the past few years, Australia. Two works of memoir (in progress) Remembering Paris and The Lucky Ones, celebrate her favourite city, Paris, and Ipswich, her childhood home. Her short story, "Death of a Show Princess", set in country Victoria, was shortlisted for the Scarlett Stiletto Awards in 2021 (Highly Commended.) Her short story, "Tough Crowd", won the Queensland Writers Centre RightLeftWrite competition in November 2021. Christine's blog, WriterPainter, rambles about Travel, Life, and Art. She is passionate about writing, animal rights, and her family.

How I got this tattoo

CHRISTINE BETTS

The notifications just keep coming.

Buzz. Buzz.

It's on silent but in the quiet space it sounds like a bullhorn. It vibrates again. This time it keeps going. A phone call. I'd just gotten comfortable, or at least as comfortable as you can get, with your forehead squashed in the face hole of a massage table.

Buzz, buzz, buzz.

I'd tried to leave the chat group, 'Bella Donna's 40th Bali Bin Fire' on WhatsApp, but then remembered I'd started the group. My sister is high maintenance, but she's got nothing on these ladies. Twenty-four women in one chat is a recipe for madness.

The vibrating of my phone stops for a moment, and I sigh. The masseuse pulls the Batik sarong down over my lower back and pours on a small amount of warm oil. It feels so good. I almost groan in pleasure. She moves her hands slowly across my back, spreading the warm oil. I am so glad I ignored my fear.

Soft instrumental music swells over the tinny speakers. I nestle down into the massage table, allowing myself a tiny sigh. The notifications start again. The phone vibrates so much it falls off my bag and onto the concrete floor, where the buzzing is amplified. I try to ignore it. As a mother of three, I should be skilled at zoning out, but I'm not. No wonder I'm so tense.

The woman in the next cubicle hisses through the Batik curtain. 'It's supposed to be switched off.'

The masseuse grabs my phone as it buzzes towards the door.

"Sorry," I mouth. My heart is pounding in my chest, but she shrugs and hands it to me like it is no big deal.

Switching the phone off, I can only think about getting the masseuse's hands on my back again, but I swipe and accidentally open the first message. I sit up and clutch the sarong to my chest.

"Oh no," I whisper. Scrolling through the dozens of messages, I look up at the concerned face of the masseuse. "I'm sorry. I have to go."

She smiles sweetly and steps out of the cubicle. I crouch down to grab my clothes and bag and pull my pants on as I tap out a quick response to the first message.

"On my way."

I glance up at the "phones on silent" sign on the wall and let out a good sigh. *I shouldn't have come to Bali. No! I should have turned the damn phone off.*

My shirt sticks to the oil on my back. I stop to take a deep breath and savour the air-conditioning for a moment longer. That woman in the next cubicle is the luckiest person in the world.

The masseuse meets me at the front desk and explains to the receptionist, a tiny, old woman with immaculately lacquered hair and nails, that I have to leave. I pull out a large note, a five hundred thousand Rupiah note, and stare at it for a moment before sliding it across the desk.

"No," the woman says and crosses her arms.

Have I just given her five dollars or fifty? I scan her face but can't tell if I've insulted her or offered her a huge tip.

"You come back later. You have full massage." She smiles and my masseuse nods.

I nearly burst into tears and glance down at my phone.

"I'm not sure I'll be back later. My sister has had … An accident." Their concerned faces nearly make me cry. The young masseuse bends behind the counter and brings out a small plastic cup of water. It has a slim white straw that she punches through the film on top. I take it gratefully and sip the cold water.

"I hope I can come back," I whisper to the masseuse as she leads the way to the front door.

I push on the door and I'm met with a wall of humid air. I dash down the steps towards the street, skimming a few more messages as I go. The security guard at the gate smiles and eyes his box of keys but looks back at me, a comically quizzical expression on his face. "You have a scooter?"

I shake my head furiously. *God, no.* "Walking." I try to smile.

He's peering at me. "You been here a short time. You have a quick massage." He mimes a very rapid shoulder massage on an invisible client.

I shake my head. "Family emergency." I wave my phone at him.

"Family here in Bali." He seems impressed.

"My sister is ahh …"

He frowns. "Is she in trouble with police … Drugs?"

I look down at my phone. There are so many messages flying back and forth I can't get a read on what's happened. "She's at the hospital."

He draws a deep, dramatic breath. "I'm sorry. I hope she's okay."

Me too.

I head out onto the footpath and search for the landmarks I memorised on the way here, not entirely confident I know the way back to the villa. I'd left early so I could take my time. It also helped that I would get to avoid my sister's intense friends for a few more hours.

The petrol station with the old phone booths out front. Check. I'm sweating. *Turn left after the statue place and the tiny closed-down cafe. Check.*

I couldn't exactly say no when my sister asked me to "organise" her big Four-Oh. That I had to arrange everything to her exact specifications was beside the point. She loved telling people her sister was overseeing her birthday celebrations. For the life of me, I couldn't work out why she wanted a yoga retreat slash gourmet cooking school slash beginner surf tour for her big birthday. She'd shown no interest in any of those things before, but since the divorce, she's been keen to try everything. She has a Bali to-do list a mile long. I only had a couple of things on my list. Massage. Cocktail. Sleep.

My husband said I should come to Bali, but I wasn't sure. I knew it would take less than a day for things to go sideways. Anything can happen with Donna, and it usually does. As it turned out, we'd only been here a few hours when the drama started. The woman who had been Donna's Chief Bridesmaid all those years ago, Cerise, fell in the pool. She was adamant someone pushed her. She was wearing her Camilla and wasn't happy. Other than me, Cerise was the only person she'd invited from her old life. The rest of the party were new friends from the gym. "Friends" should be in quotation marks because those women are fierce and not in a fun way. Who has twenty-plus close friends? Cerise has always been there for Donna, she told us when we gathered in the airport bar before our flight, even throughout her terrible marriage and divorce. I saw a couple of Donna's new friends roll their eyes at Cerise's speech, but I felt bad. Donna had pushed everyone away, so we wouldn't see what was really going on. Maybe I didn't try hard enough.

The big supermarket and the row of souvenir stores. Turn right. Check. Temple on the left opposite the café with the flags out front. Check.

The heat is killing me, but I'm impressed at how well I remember the route back to the villa. I've always had an in-built compass. Always know which way to go, in life and on the road. Sensible and boring and steady. Not Donna. Bella Donna. Dad's nickname for her stuck into adulthood. It's no surprise that her big birthday trip isn't working out as planned. Things rarely do for Donna. It isn't her fault. She's always the centre of attention, the pretty one, the social butterfly. Belladonna. Beautiful but toxic. Drama follows her like a cloud of expensive perfume.

The row of tiny shops and the restaurant with the fish tanks. Go straight. Check. Next Left.

I turn into the narrow street. I'm drenched in sweat. No one would guess that behind the high white stucco fence and traditional carved gates lies a sprawling villa with more than a dozen private bedrooms opening onto a living area and a pool. Palm trees edge the grassy yard dotted with small, thatched huts for lounging on one side and on the other by an outdoor kitchen. Donna was so happy when we got here. She cried for about ten minutes.

Three gym-friends are out front smoking.

"Where were you?" They speak in unison.

"Massage." *Not that it's any of your business.*

"Well, you picked a great time to get a massage."

Rude. "I thought a massage was a good way to start. Obviously, it was less dangerous than whatever you lot were doing."

Two of them seem shocked, but one laughs. "Who knew yoga could be so dangerous?" she says and they all giggle.

Yoga?

I walk through the tiled entryway. The fountain trickles water over the head of a Buddha statue. It's so calming and perfect, but my heart is still threatening to burst from the panic attack I am barely keeping at bay. I pause in the entry beside the fountain and put my hand to my chest. My sweaty tank top is sticking to me. I can feel the outline of my travel wallet under my clothes.

In the kitchen, Putu, our chef and cooking instructor for the week, is unpacking boxes of groceries. No one else is around. Putu wears a concerned expression and points to the hallway that leads to the room I am sharing with my sister. I wave my thanks.

The villa is quiet. Ripples of light reflecting off the pool dance on every surface. I want to throw myself into the cool water and order a cocktail from the extensive menu Putu's daughter gave us last night. I can see her through the louvred windows, chopping fruit in the outdoor kitchen.

There are three women in my room. Cerise, the Chief Bridesmaid, and two more gym-friends wearing matching crops with tiny shorts. They could be twins, or perhaps they share a cosmetic surgeon?

"Where the hell have you been?" Cerise says, eyes are red and swollen from crying. She is packing clothes into my sister's suitcase, and I remember suddenly that it was her who hardly stopped talking for the entire flight. She had an opinion on everything. At one stage, she picked up a trashy magazine with a Royal on the cover and read a two-page story out loud. In the queue for the plane toilet, I had sidled up to my sister and said, through gritted teeth, "I bet you're regretting inviting her. I'm sick of her and we haven't left Aussie airspace yet."

Donna had looked around and put her hand on my arm, leaned in and said in a whisper, "Cerise? She's got a good heart. Wouldn't

hurt a fly. She was my Chief Bridesmaid, remember, when you ...
Couldn't."

Donna always had a special knack for making me feel bad.

"I was pregnant, remember?"

Donna sighed and squeezed my arm. "And you hated my husband,
but at least we've got that in common now." I'd nudged her lightly, and
she leaned her forehead on mine like we did when we were kids. In that
moment, I actually believed the week might turn out alright.

Someone is yelling. Another voice rises. I shake my head to clear
my thoughts. My hives will start up if I stay with these women much
longer.

"Calm down, Cerise," says the one sitting on the bed, flipping
through a magazine.

I can see Cerise is about to start up, so I ask the others to leave.
"We can take it from here, me and Cerise," I say. Not that the others
were helping.

They shoot out of that room like I fired them from a gun. I watch
Cerise pack the last of Donna's clothes, the ones she had unpacked
into the generous walk-in robe only the night before. My things are
still in my bag. Takes me a while to get comfortable. Cerise's lips are
pursed, and she won't meet my eye.

"I thought she was here. The texts said she was here."

"No, they didn't. It said she was at the clinic up the road." She
shakes her head at me.

I pull out my phone to scroll through the five million messages.
I swallow hard. "If you had just sent one message, I might have
got the right information." I hold up my phone and show her the
notifications.

Cerise ignores me and folds my sister's pink swimsuit, the one she'd
bought for the trip with such a thrill of excitement. The tears that had
been sitting just behind my eyelids threaten to make an appearance.

"Such a shame she won't get to wear this," Cerise says, tucking the bikini bottom into the suitcase.

"Christ, Cerise. She's not dead."

Suddenly Cerise is in my face, her manicured finger wagging at me. "No, but now she has to turn forty while she's recovering from surgery." She glares at me.

I take a step away from the crazed banshee. "Where is she?"

"She's at the clinic, I told you. The paramedic from the consulate said she would have to be accompanied by someone responsible on the flight. I was there for her through the whole thing. She asked for me."

I shake my head. There is no way this drama queen is going to accompany Donna back to Australia.

"She's my sister. I'll take her home." My voice is soft but firm.

Cerise frowns at me for a moment, then goes back to the walk-in robe. Satisfied she has packed everything, she returns to zip the hard-shell suitcase Donna bought for the trip, her first trip overseas. Throughout her terrible marriage, she had dreamed of going to Bali. It was her only wish, something I used to think was sad. I think of her long birthday list. Bungee jumping, parasailing, learning to ride a scooter. A shiver creeps across my skin, from either the air-conditioning or my horror at riding a scooter in that traffic.

Cerise clears her throat dramatically. "It's already organised with the consulate. They've got my passport. It's done."

She heaves the suitcase off the bed, pulls out the handle and stalks from the room, towing my sister's belongings. I grab my pack, zip it up, and run the opposite way, through the utility room and out to the carpark. Voices waft from the house and Cerise appears, wheeling Donna's suitcase and her own past the fountain. I dash out the front gate. My hands are shaking as I tap the name of the clinic into Google Maps and see the little blue dot that is me, and the larger red dot that is the clinic, five hundred metres away. I shoulder my bag and start to jog. I haven't jogged since high school.

I'm a mess by the time I arrive, puffing and dripping sweat. A security guard approaches.

"My sister is here. She had an accident."

He nods his head towards the entry, and I try to catch my breath before I push the door open. Donna is sitting in the waiting area, her face bruised and bandaged. She's wearing a t-shirt that says, "I Heart Bali," but at this stage I don't think she does. I dump my bag on the cold white tiles and crouch in front of her.

I put my arm around her, carefully. "I'm so sorry. We'll have you home in no time."

"No. I want you to stay, enjoy your holiday. Your hubby got time off work to be home with the kids. He's a good man. Have a glorious holiday in my honour." Words slurring, she looks up at me with those big brown eyes. The painkillers are obviously working, but her voice is muffled and nasally. She exhales deeply and pulls a piece of paper from her pocket. "I only got one thing crossed off my list. Yoga." She pretends to check it off the list.

On the back is a line drawing of a bird leaving a domed cage. "I wanted to get this tattoo." She shrugs.

"Next time," I say. "Bella, what happened?"

She shakes her head and tries to smile. The front door of the clinic opens and Cerise bustles in with the two suitcases. Donna nods her head at her friend.

"Cerise was so keen to show off her yoga skills she broke out a Three-Legged Dog and busted my nose."

I stare at her for a moment. Cerise made me feel so guilty for not being there, and she was the culprit. Donna smooths my hair and whispers in my ear. "I asked the paramedic to tell Cerise she had to go with me. It's only fair. I want you to stay and enjoy your holiday."

I gently lean my forehead to hers and smile. Cerise is talking to the receptionist. She has the passports, and the taxi is waiting. I still feel guilty, but I'm heading straight back to the day spa to finish that massage. Donna hugs me tentatively and tucks the piece of paper in my hand.

"The only thing I ask is that you finish my list."

One week later.

I'm sure the flight attendant is smirking at me, but I'm past caring at this stage. The braids will surprise my husband, but I'll brush them out before work tomorrow. No one will believe everything, anything, I've done this week, but when I see the little bird on my wrist, I'll remember.

HARRY COLFER *is the pseudonym of an experienced critical care paramedic who lives and works in Brisbane. Although his stories are fictional, his writing style is very realistic and he maintains a healthy level of paranoia with respect to his anonymity. To date, he has published twenty-four short stories in the* Ambo Tales From The Frontline *series and plans to write another eight, one for each of the thirty-two AMPDS codes, the system used worldwide to categorise emergency calls. He has also written two novels featuring the same characters,* Dead Regular *and* Beneath Contempt, *with* High Acuity *and* Show Cause *in preparation.*

His dream is to own two homes, one in Queensland for the winter, and one in Tasmania for the summer, sailing between them on an annual migration.

He currently has one house in Brisbane and no boat, but as he says, "You have to start somewhere".

Exposure

HARRY COLFER

Our foamy wake churned and boiled behind us like a liquid contrail, tracing back to the channel markers at the marina's entrance. It was a glorious blue-sky morning, and I had to pinch myself as I hung onto the grab rail standing at the back deck of the Volunteer Marine Rescue vessel. Was an Intensive Care Paramedic needed to ferry an intoxicated man from Moreton Island? No, but who cares? It meant I was getting paid to be on a boat and I couldn't help but smile. The sea was part of me, part of my childhood, part of my psyche. If I had a soul, it would be awash with saline.

I caught sight of a Pied Cormorant tracing the surface of the bay, flying a metre or two above the undulating waters like a feathered Exocet missile. Following the bird's progress, my view was led inside the cabin, and all the joy evaporated. My crewmate, Ed Roberts, was fast asleep on a bench, hands clasped in front of his rotund belly, head bobbing with every wave. Lasting a twelve-hour shift with him was always a challenge. Our energy levels and outlooks were at opposite ends of the spectrum.

One of the deckies came out to join me. Like many of the VMR staff, he was of retirement age, grey-haired and well-meaning. He nodded at Ed. "Is he OK?" He glanced at his watch. "Are you guys finishing off a night shift?"

I laughed. "No, we're both as fresh as a daisy, but don't worry, sleeping is Ed's superpower. You've heard of Time Lords? Well, Ed's a 'Sleep Lord'."

The aged deckhand frowned at me and I decided to change the subject. "So, where's Shark Spit? I've been to Moreton plenty of times, but haven't heard of it."

He shrugged as he reached up to hold the grab rail. "That's because there's not much there." He nodded to himself and I thought he'd stopped talking. "It's a point on the leeward side ... 'Bout halfway between Tangalooma and the Big Sandhills ... Y'know, the nearer of those sandy patches over there."

He pointed with his free hand to the two rips in the island's foliage. His voice was a slow drawl from lips that seemed reluctant to move. I had to lean close to hear him over the noise of the twin outboards.

"It's marked by a couple of old wrecks ... The Normanby and The Fairlight ... Not much to see of them, though ... The Fairlight was a paddle steamer ... Used to be the pride of the Port Jackson Steamship Company ... Ferried folk between Sydney and Manly in luxury ... All that remains now is a few girders and a rusty boiler ... People pass by without a second glance ... Decades of dedicated service ... Discarded and left to rot on the sand."

His voice tailed off as he gazed into the distance with rheumy eyes, and I wasn't sure if he was still talking about the shipwreck. We swayed in unison for a few minutes, hanging from the overhead bar like commuters on a bus, until my need-to-talk threshold was breached. "Oh, by the way, I'm Jono and Sleeping Beauty in there is Ed."

He nodded and for a moment I thought he wouldn't reciprocate. "Earl."

I smiled back. "Nice to meet you, Earl."

"Likewise." Another pause. "The skipper's Murray." He turned towards the helm, as if to remind himself who was on board. "The guy next to him is Bob."

"Right. You been doing this long?"

"Only a few years ... Keeps me on the water."

Once again, we lapsed into another awkward silence. Awkward for me, that is. Earl seemed quite comfortable with staccato sentences interspersed with pregnant pauses.

I adjusted my sunnies. "Not much boat traffic out for such a wonderful day."

He swivelled his head around like a slow radar to check my assessment. "True." Another long engine-drone silence. "It's Tuesday."

I glanced at my watch for confirmation, the rolling-shift-worker's constant affliction.

"They posted a weather warning a few days ago ... Got it wrong ... Again."

Despite the wonderful vista, the smell of sea spray, and the warmth of the morning sun, I considered waking Ed to avoid a further stilted conversation. But then Earl began pottering around the deck, rearranging ropes, fenders, and various pieces of equipment for no apparent reason. I sighed in relief and turned to view the approaching shoreline.

Up ahead, I could make out the shape of Moreton's four-wheel-drive ambulance, a Toyota Troop Carrier, crewed by one of the two luckiest paramedics in the Brisbane City Ambulance Service. They got to live at the island's resort for a week and then spent a similar time back home. Although they worked alone, the caseload could hardly be described as taxing.

I could also see the rusted wrecks Earl had mentioned, but anchored nearby in the shallows was a far more modern vessel. Sunlight glinted off the brilliant white hull of a dagger-like ski boat that had colourful lettering along its flanks, and a huge outboard sitting on the transom. As the VMR engine tone calmed, we cruised closer, and I was not surprised to read 'Bogan Blitz' emblazoned in graffiti-style writing.

A female paramedic was waiting on the shore, arms folded and hips cocked to one side. Her blonde hair was tied in a ponytail fed through the back of her cap, and she watched us through over-sized dark sunglasses.

My face broke into a grin as I recognised her and I unzipped my boots, took them and my socks off, and rolled up my pants. The skipper came out of the cabin and frowned as he saw me. "I was just about to say someone's going to have to wade to shore, but I guess you've done this before."

"Many times in my own boat, but usually you guys take us to the jetty."

"True. That'd be the simplest option, but seeing as we've just got word the patient's still unconscious, the island's paramedic will need help. If you load the patient in their Troopie, we can meet at Tangalooma."

"Sounds like a plan. Ed can stay with you and look after our kit."

We all turned to see him draped on the bench, his bushy moustache quivering with each breath. The skipper raised an eyebrow.

"Don't be fooled by his apparent relaxed state. If anyone touches our gear, he'll pounce like a ninja."

Without opening his eyes, Ed raised his middle finger.

"See."

The skipper shrugged. "Whatever, over you go. Can you give the bow a push as you leave? I've brought us in as close as I can."

Agreeing, I swung myself over the gunwale and lowered my feet into the crystal clear waters, the golden sand rolling back and forth with the gentle action of the breaking waves. After helping them to free their vessel, I turned and waded to shore, opening my arms wide in a welcome. "Ducky! Fancy meeting you here."

She grinned and shook her head. "Jono! Long time no see, mate. What the hell have they sent you for?"

"Heard you were struggling here in paradise. Thought you might need someone to help clean the sand off your boots."

"Right. Great use of an ICP, but hey, always glad to see you."

I knew Ducky, aka Anna, from her student days, but had lost touch since she qualified. I joined her on the dry sand above the strandline and was looking around for our patient. "So, what've you got for me? I've heard you've found some intox bloke."

"Yep, yep, yep. He's up here under the trees. At least he had the sense to sit in the shade before getting shitfaced. I'm just amazed someone spotted him."

We were trudging up the soft sand and onto the first sprigs of vegetation that helped to stop the entire island from disappearing into the sea. Underneath the spiky fronds of a sprawling pandanus palm was the body of a man in his thirties, attached to a monitor that was beeping out a rhythm and displaying a set of vitals, all within the normal range. From our elevated position, I turned around and could see the VMR vessel carving out a white line through the turquoise waters and heading off towards the resort. "Who the hell found him?"

"Some adventurous tourists took a morning stroll down the beach to see the wrecks. They came up here for the shade."

I laughed. "Earl will be pleased."

"Who?"

"Dunna worry. So, he's really unconscious, then?"

"Yep, yep, yep. A solid GCS 3, blood sugar's normal, before you ask. I've tried everything, all the tricks you taught me, even inserted an NP airway, but nothing."

"Mind if I try to elicit a response?"

"Be my guest."

I bent over our patient, who was wearing the obligatory singlet, shorts, and thongs. He had sun-darkened skin and his face bore a boatie's tan, pale racoon eyes from the permanent use of sunnies. As I pushed my fist down onto his sternum, I couldn't help notice his chunky gold necklace that must have been worth a fortune. Thirty seconds of hard, unrelenting pressure failed to summon the slightest reaction. "Wow. A definite GCS 3. I agree, he's unconscious."

"Told you."

"I guess it could be a stroke, or perhaps a GHB overdose?"

Ducky pouted. "I reckon it's alcohol." She pointed to two empty litre bottles of Jack Daniels lying in the undergrowth.

"Jesus. I'm not surprised he's still comatose. D'you think he owns that boat out there?"

"What, the Bogan Blitz? Could do."

"It'd explain how he got here and also give us an ID." I checked his pockets. There was no wallet, but a boat key on a float. "Bingo."

"Well, seeing as the VMR has left, are you going to swim out there just to determine his name? I'm sure as hell not taking a dip for him."

I gave it a moment's thought. "John Doe it is, then. So, should we drag him on a carry sheet down to your stretcher?"

She started disconnecting the monitoring. "Yep, yep, yep. I think it's our only option. Where's your crewmate, anyway?"

I sighed. "I'm working with Ed."

She nodded. "Sleeping?"

"Got it in one."

"Probably best he's not here. We wouldn't want two patients. I'll go get the carry sheet."

We dragged Mr Doe over the sand on the thick plastic sheet and were both sweating by the time we had him loaded in the ambulance. I climbed in the back. "Get that aircon on!"

"Here, less of your whinging." She threw me a bottle of chilled water and fired up the engine, causing blessed cool air to flow from the cab.

"Thanks. Next stop Tangalooma, but any chance we can go the long way round?"

"I'd love to, Jono, but even these Troopies are tracked. They'd be onto us within minutes."

"Damn, should have known Big Brother would be watching."

She nodded and picked up the mic as we set off. "Comms, this is Moreton Island, patient loaded and proceeding to meet with VMR at the jetty."

"Roger that, Moreton."

"Keeping them informed? That's very good of you, Ducky. What's happened?"

"Simple. I'm on a gig that I don't want to lose."

"Totally understand. I might even toe the line if I was out here. I reckon when I tire of the city I'll go work somewhere near a beach. Gotta make the rough smoother."

"Yep, yep, yep!"

The journey to the resort grounds only took a few minutes, and we were soon climbing out of the Troopie at the end of the jetty. Ed was waiting with Earl and Bob.

"Found someone who can rival your sleeping prowess, Ed. I reckon you should compete in a sleep-off. My money's on you."

"Up yours."

The five of us grabbed the handles of the carry sheet and manhandled Mr Doe onto the boat's stretcher before saying our goodbyes and casting off from the jetty.

As we motored away from the island, our patient groaned and pulled out the long nasopharyngeal airway from his nose. I turned and held his shoulder. "Hey, mate. What's your name?"

He pushed his body up from the stretcher and looked around, as if he'd just beamed aboard a starship. "W … Wha …? Where the fuck am I?"

"You've been picked up by the Volunteer Marine Rescue. You were found unconscious on a beach at Moreton Island."

He rubbed his face then massaged the mullet at the back of his neck. "Moreton? Shit. Where's m' boat?"

"Is that the Bogan Blitz?"

He grinned. "Yer. If the shoe fits, fuckin' wear it."

I had to laugh at his unexpected self-deprecation. "It's anchored where you left it, mate, Shark Spit."

His eyes grew wide, and he placed a hand on his mouth. "Oh shit! What day is it?"

Again, I glanced at my watch. "Tuesday."

"Tuesday! Shit, shit, shit! Oh God no!"

He was getting agitated, and I thought he might be having a flashback. "Calm down, you're all good. You're safe now."

"No, no, you don't understand! I was only supposed to be killing a few hours on Moreton. It's me brother! He gave me a couple of bottles of JD to drop him and his missus off on Green Island. Shit! That was yestdee mornin'!"

The gravity of the situation dawned on me. "Did they have any water?"

"Only one bottle each, nothin' else. Shit, nothin' else! Oh my God, he's going to kill me."

I was more concerned about the two people left on a tiny island exposed to the elements for over twenty-four hours. "D'you have his home number? They might have flagged down another boat."

"Sure."

We were close enough to the mainland for mobile coverage, and I called the number he recited. "I need your name and theirs?"

"I'm Shane, he's Dwayne and she's Britney."

"Right. OK, there's no answer. Skipper, can we swing by Green Island? We might have two more patients."

"Already diverted. Can you inform your guys what's happening?"

"On it." I grabbed the wall-mounted mic and hit the transmit button as the engine tone kicked up a notch or two. "Comms, this is 942 on the VMR. We've just had a report of two more potential patients on Green Island. As we're on the water, we're going to take a look."

"Roger that, 942. Keep us posted."

"Will do."

Tension mounted aboard the boat — even Ed managed to stay awake — as the skipper unleashed the twin 250-horsepower outboards and we flew over the water. The low-lying expanse of Mud Island was soon passing on our starboard side, followed by St Helena with its ruined penal colony. But our focus was on the tiny mangrove-covered bump dead ahead. We were aiming for the sandy beach on the northern tip, and as we approached, two figures stood and started waving in our direction. Coming closer, we realised they were butt naked, their exposed appendages wiggling around in time with their gesticulations. We all turned to look at Shane.

"I did say they had nothin' else. They're 'Survivor' nuts. They wanted to experience being shipwrecked for a few hours."

Ed stared at the spectacle. "Well, that ain't something you'd see on TV."

I frowned, mesmerised by the jiggling. "I think they'd definitely cut this scene from the show. Have we got sheets and plenty of water?"

Earl started rummaging through lockers and eskies. "I'll get it sorted."

Desperate to be rescued, they somehow found enough energy to swim the short distance to the boat, and we eased them aboard, being careful to avoid touching their skin, which was red raw, blistered, and covered in sandfly bites. Britney had to be helped onto the stretcher, where she all but passed out, and Dwayne lay on the bench, spent after his recent exertion, but staring at his brother with murderous intent. Shane retreated to the back deck as Ed and I got to work on our new patients, gaining intravenous access, and attempting to remedy their heat exposure and dehydration with sips of water and saline infusions.

Although they looked awful, having been feasted on by insects all night, their obs were reasonable given the circumstances. I left them with Ed to go check on Shane. "Are you coming with us to hospital?"

"Nah. Don't think that's a smart idea. I'm sure I've had worse hangovers. I reckon I'd better stay away from me brother for a while."

I nodded. "You're probably right."

"I've somehow got to get back to me boat."

"Well, I'll leave you to sort that out."

I returned inside and grabbed the radio. "Comms, this is 942. We now have a total of two patients, so could you please send a second ambulance to meet us at the VMR dock?"

"Roger, 942, will do."

After motoring up to Scarborough, the skipper eased off on the revs and we chugged into the marina, Earl and Bob securing the vessel to its own dedicated berth. Shane hovered in the background as we assisted a sheet-covered Dwayne to his feet and out onto the deck. He was about to step off the boat when his sibling approached. "I'm so sorry, bro. I hope you get better soon." And without thinking, he patted his back.

Dwayne roared in agony, and despite his exhaustion, spun round, catching his brother under the chin with a ferocious uppercut. There was a slap sound, like Rocky's fist on a meat carcass, and Shane hit the deck with all the grace of a loose cowpat. Showing no regret, his brother turned and staggered off down the quay, leaving us all staring in his wake.

Checking Shane was still breathing, I reached inside the cabin and retrieved the mic. "Er ... Comms, this is 942. Our original patient is unconscious again. Apologies, but we're going to need a third ambulance."

MARINA HACQUIN is a writer based in Southern Tasmania. She writes about issues that resonate with youth including the environment, social justice and health. She is inspired by people, nature, travel and books.

Australia's Ark

MARINA HACQUIN

The green spot wandered through the luminous Tasmanian sky. Holding my breath, I realised it was rapidly losing height. In my right hand, I held my *Field Guide to Tasmanian Birds*. I didn't need to open it, though — I had recognised the fast, direct flight and the bright colours of the Swift Parrot.

I moved my face closer to the window. I could see a layer of condensation taking shape on the glass. A high-pitch call resonated in the room, loud and clear as the bird perched on the edge of the window. Our eyes met. There was something oddly moving about its appearance, red around the bill and throat as if it had plunged half its face in a jar of strawberry jam. I stroked the glass with my fingertips and closed my eyes, imagining the softness of its feathers.

"Elliott, it's dinner time! Mum said to turn off the *SmartWindow!*" shouted Lizzie, bringing me back to reality.

I opened my eyes. The moving picture of the Tasmanian wilderness had been replaced by a blue screen. The Swift Parrot was gone.

Her hand still on the switch of the *SmartWindow*, Lizzie stood there with a smirk on her face.

I tightened my grip on my book. Another day in lockdown had passed, similar to the previous one, identical to the next. Stuck in an emergency accommodation somewhere underneath the city of Melbourne, I was condemned to watch videos of birds on a screen.

However, as I rested my head on my pillow that night, recalling the memory of my virtual encounter with the feathered creature, I realised that a spark of hope had ignited within me.

...

I was born in Tasmania during a freezing winter, only weeks before it became an official no-go zone. Some said it had become a refuge island for the wealthy. Others believed the state's closure was a necessary sacrifice to keep Australia's flora and fauna sheltered from human activity and the ravages of climate change on the mainland. Worldwide, the island was known as Australia's Ark. Like many other families, we had been forced to relocate to Victoria. All we had left of our time living there were videos of our explorations of the Southwest Wilderness, which I avidly watched on the *SmartWindow* during my free time. This, and a mysterious message scribbled on the back of an envelope:

> To find your South dreams, you need to find the moving River first
> Wilson will dive you the anser.

"An old fisherman gave it to Mum when we disembarked from the Spirit of Tasmania in Melbourne on its last voyage," Dad had told me a few years back. "He was a nice bloke; we'd spent a few hours talking about our wild adventures." He didn't know what it meant, but he had kept it all these years for its sentimental value.

I missed Dad. He had always been my hero and wore his firefighting uniform with pride. He had fought countless bushfires and helped rehome thousands of people displaced by Cyclone Seth in Brisbane. A few weeks ago, he had been called to his duty once again — this time, two blazes threatened the outskirts of Melbourne, including the suburb in which we lived. Unable to escape by road or air, we had been relocated to an underground safety apartment complex built by the government. It was small, dark and smelly, but safe.

At breakfast, Mum seemed preoccupied. I noticed dark patches under her eyes. She hadn't turned on the radio for days, so I had no idea how things were unfolding outside.

"Mum, when can we go outside? I learnt ten new species of birds, and I want to find them in the wild," I asked softly.

"With the fires that are consuming the forests, there won't be any left," giggled Lizzie.

"That's not true. Dad and his friends will stop them," I retorted.

"You think you live in a utopia," Lizzie quipped.

"You think using complicated words makes you sound clever, but it doesn't," I replied.

"Utopia is not a complicated word. It is just rarely used because people are scared to talk about their dreams."

I opened my mouth to tell her about my desire to return to Tasmania but said nothing. Could she be right? We finished breakfast in a deafening silence.

After completing my homework, I went to the living room, the only place equipped with a *SmartWindow*. I was longing for nature, and with the help of my *Field Guide*, I was hoping to spot a Tasmanian Azure Kingfisher and a Forty-spotted Pardalote in some of Mum and Dad's earlier videos.

I pressed the switch. Nothing happened. I tried again, but the screen remained desperately black. I was about to walk out when the emergency phone on the wall went off in a blare. I picked it up hesitantly.

"Elliott, listen to me." It was Dad's voice. He sounded out of breath, and my heart started racing.

"Dad?"

"Take the masks, fill up the water container, wet all our towels in the bath, grab the emergency backpack and get out of here," he urged.

"Get out of the underground? Are the fires over?"

Dad started coughing. Voices were screaming in the background. A sense of foreboding started creeping up on me.

"Dad, what's wrong?"

Mum appeared at the doorstep carrying the emergency backpack, her eyes wide open in terror. Behind her, Lizzie was crying. Mum took the phone off my hands, and my body started shaking. I saw Mum's lips move, pressing the phone against her ear as tears rolled down her cheeks. My legs carried me to the bathroom as if they were driven with a will of their own and I proceeded to collect the masks, fill up our water can and wet some towels. Just like Dad said.

As we watched the garage door of the underground car park lift, I hugged my *Field Guide* against my heart. We saw a dim light filtering through the dust particles behind the car's windows as we drove through an eerie landscape. It reminded me of when we had found ourselves shrouded in a dust storm in the state's north. Dad had stopped the car and started singing songs, one after another, until the sky had reclaimed its position above our heads.

But this time, it was different. It wasn't a dust storm. And Dad wasn't here.

There was a loud *bang*. Something had fallen on our windscreen. Through the dust, I glimpsed the shape of a yellow wing. My heart skipped a beat.

"Mum, the bird! We need to save it! Stop!" I screamed with a croaky voice.

I could see its little body slide up and down in rhythm with the windscreen wipers. Up. The smell of smoke. Down. The roaring engine. Up. The belt pressing against my neck. Down. Mum's hands clasping the steering wheel. Up. A metallic taste in my mouth.

Unable to watch this gruesome spectacle any longer, I replaced my face mask, released my seatbelt and opened the door.

Mum's scream got lost in the distance as the heat and the dust hit me all at once. I fell on the side of the road and the car stopped. Keeping my left hand on the car's body, I progressed to the front of the vehicle, gently cupped my hands around the bird and ran back inside the car, coughing. Mum didn't say anything, but I heard the sound of the child safety lock being activated. Lizzie's face was livid. My eyes stung so much I closed them, and I groped for her hand, which I held until I fell asleep, the bird resting on the wet towels stacked in between us.

When I opened my eyes, Mum was sobbing quietly on the driver's seat; a large Australian road atlas opened on her lap. The blue of the sky was still nowhere to be seen, but the dust cover was thinner, and sunlight was breaking through. I slid my frail body to the passenger's seat.

"I don't know what to do or where to go, my love. And I don't know where your daddy is. I am so sorry."

At the mention of Dad, I started crying. Mum stroked my face gently before kissing my forehead.

"Where are we now?" I asked, holding back my tears.

Mum pointed to the coast east of Melbourne. A detail caught my attention. The Wilson Promontory National Park, situated only a few dozen kilometres from our location, sounded familiar. I recited the fisherman's message from the top of my head.

To find your South dreams, you need to find the moving River first
Wilson will dive you the anser.

Following the atlas' instructions, I opened to page 33 for a detailed map of the national park. As I was going through the map, I found what I was looking for.

South Point is the southernmost point on the Australian mainland.

The next page had a more detailed breakdown of the area:

South Point is situated 4.5 km east of Anser Island.
Tidal River is a popular campground within the park.

Mum and I exchanged a long stare.

"It was ten years ago, Elliott. It's nonsense; we don't know for sure that the fisherman was referring to the Tidal River. It could have been a mistake. He even wrote *dive* instead of *give.*"

"Dad always believed it had some sort of meaning. He was right! Let's go to Tidal River. This is our way back to Tasmania."

"This is madness. The island is guarded by the military. Besides, it is a conservation area; there are no industries, no schools, no nothing."

"Do you think growing up breathing ashes and living underground is a better option?" cried Lizzie, who had just woken up.

Mum blinked twice. There was a glimmer of hope in her tired eyes; I could see it now.

"Mum, oh, Mum," I begged. "Please."

She bit her lip, and tears filled her eyes. I was holding my breath when she finally spoke:

"If we can't find anything there, we will drive to the South East underground complex."

. . .

We drove in silence through a devastated landscape, Lizzie and I pressing our noses against the dirty windows while chewing stale bread Mum had found at the bottom of the emergency backpack.

"I spy with my little eye," Lizzie began after a while, but it was all just blackened trees and dirt, so we blew warm air on the glass and drew animals with our fingers.

By the time we reached Tidal River Township, the smoke had cleared. I had spread breadcrumbs around the bird, whose sleeping body was jolting with the bumps in the road. According to my *Field Guide*, it was a male Golden Whistler, a virtuoso singer with a golden plumage and a black hood. Lizzie believed it was dead, but I could feel its heartbeat.

We drove past the visitor centre, and Mum parked the car in front of the general store. She turned to me to say something, but when she saw Lizzie was asleep, she pressed her finger on her lips and disappeared inside the wooden building. The window was half open and I poked my head through, letting the sea breeze fill my lungs and throat until I felt dizzy. *Escuro & Sons Diving School, 5km,* said a crumbling sign across the street.

When Mum returned from the information centre, she had regained composure and her face exuded determination. She pointed to the sign and declared:

"This is where we are going. They said a man there could help us."

We were back on the road. I closed my eyes from relief and exhaustion and rested my fingers on the bird. A wave of sadness swept my heart upon feeling its pulseless body. Muffled sobs became cries of grief, and my face flooded with tears. I wanted to get out but the door was locked.

"Let me out!"

Mum stopped the car, unlocked the doors, and I rushed out of the vehicle with Lizzie on my heels. A few metres away, sheltered by a giant eucalyptus tree, an ageless man was sitting outside a derelict building on which the words *Escuro & Sons Diving School* had been crudely painted.

"We are closed to visitors." His beard was so thick I could not see his mouth.

"We want to sail past Anser Island," I requested. "Back to Tasmania."

The man kept staring at me but said nothing. I paused on his name tag; my eyes blurred with tears.

"Please ... Will Jr?"

...

We embarked on the dive boat in the early morning, on the eve of Lizzie's birthday, my *Field Guide* carefully packaged in a waterproof bag. We had left a letter for Dad at the shack but, deep inside me, I knew he would sense what had happened and follow our tracks. Will Jr, the son of the fisherman who had met my parents on their journey across the Bass Strait channel, told us that families had illegally returned to the island since its closure, but what had happened to them, no one knew for sure.

We didn't know what we would find in Tasmania, but we knew what we were leaving behind, and that was enough. And perhaps, when I would be as strong and brave as Mum and Dad, one day, I would explore the Southwest Wilderness of Tasmania and come face to face with a real Swift Parrot.

MELANIE KANICKY *is a writer from Melbourne with a special interest in young adult and speculative fiction. Her short stories have appeared in anthologies such as* Thresholds *and the* Wyndham Writing Awards Anthology *(2021). She is completing her Master's in Writing and Literature at Deakin University, with a focus in Creative Writing. She hopes to have her own novels published one day, but for now she works full time managing a bustling bookstore in Melbourne's eastern suburbs.*

Salt for cleansing

MELANIE KANICKY

It was the first Tuesday of August on the isle of Harpsmoor, which meant someone was going to die.

Arnold knew it as well as any of the other townsfolk, who gathered in their homes with the curtains drawn tight and whispered by the light of their fireplaces, waiting for the sun to rise over the sea.

No one slept in. Not on the first Tuesday of August.

Who would it be? They asked themselves. Who would walk — compelled, dreamlike — into the foaming waves and not return? Last year it had been Thomas Milligan, a lad scarcely old enough to grow hair on his chin. Mrs Milligan had watched him do it.

She hadn't dared scream out to stop him. What good would it have done, to drag him away from that beach, away from the dark, pocked rocks, and the gulls that cried overhead? She could save him from one stretch of beach, but the island was bordered by naught but sea. The boy would have found his way there eventually.

Everyone did.

Better to let him go, fast and quick, into the surf that rose and fell like a mother's sobbing breast. The tides would get him, dragging and stealing and feasting, and it would be done.

None of the others helped. They watched, grim-faced, as Mrs Milligan's heart crumbled alone on the foreshore, clutching at their families and secretly gladdened that it was not their own son over there, breathing down the brine. The wind buffeted their church skirts, blew away their best hats, and coated them all with salted air. Under their breaths, they whispered as one:

Salt for cleansing, sea for birthing.

Arnold had stood alone, far from the group, in sodden gumboots and unwashed trousers. He'd lived on Harpsmoor for thirty-two years, and still he had no answers. What was birthed, out there in the waves, with decades of the dead strewn across the ocean floor? What good was salt for cleansing, if those who walked into the sea no longer had sins to care for?

Perhaps the salt was not meant for the dead.

. . .

Island life was not for everyone. Arnold was loath to admit it, but the folk of Harpsmoor were just as grizzled and hardened as the mainlanders suspected. Life was harder on the island. *A bit backwards*, they said. Families raised their own meat, mostly chicken and geese, and a few cows — there was not enough good grass to support anything more — and no child cowered at the thought of slaughtering their own meal. The chickens were not beloved pets, though the folk might love their eggs and tender meat. They served a purpose, just as the chosen who marched into the sea served a purpose. It was not a topic discussed at dinner tables or whispered over pillows, but it was not shied from. It was worn with a stiff upper lip, and the stoop of shoulders that had seen too much loss.

What choice was there but to move forward, or drown with the weight of it all?

A select few homes had televisions, though the reception was so poor that it was hardly worth the electricity. The tower, high up on the northern hill, had been damaged in a storm. Someone many years ago, their name long since swallowed up, had written to the technicians on the mainland, but none had ever come.

Children were few and far between. Many of the islanders were too old to bear them, or their own children had been gobbled down before grandchildren could come screaming into the world. Arnold sometimes wondered if the year would come when there was no one left to take. What would happen then? How long would it take for the mainlanders to learn that the island was abandoned? They would not know about the hungry sea – they would come, and they would build and expand, and invite tourists to pay to stay in shining hotels. And every year, someone would die, and there would be nobody left to hold their hands and sit them down, and murmur gentle words to them.

Salt for cleansing, sea for birthing.

...

Only the most tenacious of the townsfolk kept a garden. They had to be militant, for even the earth was salted here, and would try to burn and shrivel the plants from the roots up. Shabby walls were erected to protect their harvests from the endless, pummelling winds, and generational friendships had been built upon an agreement to share vegetable scraps and manure for compost. At the end of the season, their work was rewarded with a small bounty. Beets in winter, asparagus in spring, spinach in autumn, and a scant few sour tomatoes in the summer.

Arnold hated beets. He hated the way the pink juice stained everything it touched, how they tasted of the earth, and how they reminded him of Tilly. A vegetable, Arnold maintained, had no business dredging up ghosts.

What the townspeople couldn't grow or make themselves was brought to Harpsmoor on a ferry that arrived every four weeks, bearing everything from baking flour to Band-Aids, stocked with newspapers from the mainland that were dated before they arrived. Nothing went to waste, and though Arnold doubted anyone read the news, the papers were kept in neat stacks and used to sop up spills, or pulled apart, scrunched into tight balls, and lit to stoke a reluctant fire. Sometimes the ink would burn green, just for a moment.

It had been Martin, first, who had handled the logistics of the ferry, using the island's only phone to call in and book the deliveries, collating the handwritten lists of what the residents needed and ordering accordingly. But Martin had been gone for five years, and now the task was on a rotating roster. It had been one of his ferries that had brought Arnold to the island, more than three decades ago, and Martin who had pulled Arnold aside and asked him if he was certain he wanted to stay.

Of course, Arnold had answered. *Even islands need guidance.*

The church was built high on the hill that overlooked the bluffs, next to the crumbling lighthouse that had not been used, perhaps, ever. The white tower's paint had been cracked and peeled even back then, but Arnold had taken it as a sign. If the beacon was not lit to guide ships through the rocks, perhaps it was meant to be used in service of driving the misguided into his hallowed hall for penance and wisdom, faith and devotion. A white pillar to match the white collar he wore around his neck.

But the days of filled services were gone. Arnold had arrived in the spring, and sermoned until the winter, when it became clear that there was no room for faith on Harpsmoor. Something else was already there. Something else already had a claim on these souls, and it could not be broken, or bartered with, or prayed away. At least, Arnold told himself, he had met Tilly. Martin's daughter. They'd had twenty-eight good years together. After Martin walked into the spray, though, something in Arnold's wife had broken. It was only two years later that it came back for her. Perhaps the ocean had known, somehow, that grief had killed her long before it pulled her down.

Salt for cleansing, sea for birthing.

This first Tuesday of August marked the third anniversary of Tilly's death, and Arnold was ready. The first year he had been so lost that he hadn't even noticed the passing date. He woke, and ambled down to the beach to watch without even realising he was doing it. Someone had led him home to his stone cottage by the church, and laid him down on his bed with a glass of whiskey beside him. Then of course, last year, Thomas Milligan had been taken, so early that the sky was still dark, and the waves had whisked him away before Arnold could throw himself in their path.

This year would be different.

Arnold didn't let himself sleep that night. He paced the house, touching a drawing Tilly had done one summer when the sky was clear and the ocean calm. It was a landscape, overlooking the sea and the cliffs from their private perch on the hill, and every stroke of the pencil had been rendered with grace and precision. She had loved the island, loved the sea and the salt even though Arnold found nothing there worth loving. What did that say about him?

Finally, night receded its grip, and the stars began to fade. Arnold left the cottage, closing the door with care and laying the key beneath a shrivelled pot plant. Someone would find it. He trudged past the church, not daring to glance at it, and circumvented the lighthouse.

This was where Tilly had stood and drawn, the likeness captured so perfectly that Arnold imagined himself, just for a moment, stuck in time and graphite, unchanging and endless, borne by his wife's own hand.

Arnold scrubbed his face and found it wet.

There was a single track that wove down the hill towards the beach, carved away from years of feet. Arnold maundered down, not quite seeing, not quite feeling. Always, the sound of the ocean filled his ears, but today it was louder. It was too dark to make out much, save the white foam, and the darkened shadows of jutting black rocks.

The sea always knew. No matter how far it receded, it always came back.

Late winter wind howled against Arnold's ears, biting and angry. As he climbed further down the hill, a hint of sunlight flickered over the horizon, illuminating the outline of dark, full clouds. It would rain later. There was nothing, Arnold thought, more lovely than rain on the sea. He would not see it today, but he would not be in want of water anyway.

The climb down the hills set the old ache in his knee aflame. Arnold was an old man now, face weathered and weary, hair grey and patchy. His knuckles were perpetually swollen and red. His stomach and arms had grown flabby, skin sagging, and his vision was marred by a small blurry patch in his left eye that remained no matter how much he tried to blink it away.

Even with his sight encumbered, Arnold didn't miss the fuzzy outline of figures approaching from the town. They walked in a line as soldiers might, following the stumbling, clumsy shape of one another.

Arnold's breath hitched. Someone had been roused from their slumber, called to, from across the cliffs and bluff and tufts of thick grass, by a wordless, soundless voice on the wind. They answered the call, and the townsfolk knew it. Which of them would grieve the most, but pretend not to, and which would hurry home to their children, and tell them that they were lucky they were such well-behaved children, that the sea would never ask such a thing of them?

Who would lie the most convincingly?

Arnold begged his aging legs to carry him faster down the slope. The others would know, now that they had seen the chosen somnambulantly creeping towards the edge of their life, that Arnold was not called to. Not like that.

He had to hope that the sea would understand. A life freely given, surely, was just as sweet as one plucked from their bed.

The first gulls of the morning began to stir, cawing and screeching as they ducked to and fro, searching for something tasty that had washed up on the shore. Even the sun began to rouse itself properly, and the dark sky turned a hollow grey.

Arnold reached the end of his path, and swathes of black rock and washed-out sand greeted him. The stumbling figure was still a hundred metres back, approaching from the north-west. There was time enough for Arnold to shuck off his jacket and remove his shoes and socks. Someone could use them after he was gone, and there was no sense in taking them with him.

Arnold took the last step off the rock and onto the shore. The sand was wet and freezing, and his feet sunk deep as though the land itself was not ready to yield him over. But Arnold had survived on the island for three decades, and the land was not what held sway over him anymore. He marched the path he had watched countless others traverse without thought. Always, they entered from the same spot on the shore, following a guiding line of obsidian stone.

The first lap of shallow water greeted his toes, testing, tasting. The shock of cold almost had him skipping backwards. Away, away, away.

Arnold sucked in a last breath of briny air, tasting the sea and drying seaweed, the sickly sweet of something rotting.

The sound of crying chased him further into the depths. The tears were not meant for him.

Arnold's shins were submerged, and his teeth chattered in the cold. Steeling himself, he gazed out into the same waters that had claimed Tilly, Martin, young Thomas and thirty more still. He gritted his teeth. He was not afraid.

But——

Something moved in the sea. Arnold caught a glimpse, then it was gone beneath the waves again. Squinting, he leaned forward, certain his eyes were playing one final trick on him.

There.

Through the rising water, something hovered beyond the sandbank. Pale, bobbing, flailing.

Arnold froze. He watched as the bobbing, pale thing hoisted itself up onto the shoal. The sky grew lighter, the waves began to calm, and there, dripping, bloated, eyes clouded, was a woman. She unfurled herself and stood tall, and Arnold's breath caught in his chest.

Tilly.

His wife's eyes were clouded, and her whiting hair was plastered to her scalp. More water than seemed feasible was pouring off her, but Arnold knew it was Tilly beneath her bloated, grey skin. She wore her favourite night dress, the one Arnold knew she had died in, only now it was torn, and seaweed clung to the buttons in limp ribbons. Through the rips, Tilly's skin was mottled and purple.

His wife turned, and her pale, foggy eyes sought out Arnold's.

It was only then that Arnold noticed her stomach. It bulged, pushing against the fabric of her dress, round with the child that they had never had. With the child Tilly was far too old to carry.

Around him, the sea crashed and waned, pushing and pulling his body through the surf. The cold was a faraway thing as Arnold watched his wife rest a hand against her stomach, tender and sweet. Her fingers stuck out at odd angles. Twisted. Wrong.

Arnold's wife smiled, and salt water streamed through her teeth. It dribbled over her lips and chin, pouring back into the sea in which they stood.

Behind him, the wailing stopped. A chorus struck up on the shore.

Salt for cleansing, sea for birthing.

PIPPA KAY *lives in Sydney NSW and has sailed extensively on her yacht*
Renaissance *with her husband. She is a member of the Coastal Cruising Club of*
Australia and edits their newsletter, Mainsheet. *Pippa is the author of three books,*
the most recent being a collection of short stories published by Ginninderra Press called
Keeping it in the Family. *This book won the Society of Women Writers Fiction*
Award in 2018.

Unwanted goods

PIPPA KAY

The bearded, tattooed man they called Tug left the yacht club,
following a trail of garden lights that led to the marina. Behind him,
the band played *American Pie*, and ahead he heard rigging thwacking
against masts and the slap of sea against hulls.

"Okay, if that's the way you want it, then ..." he muttered to
himself ... *then he would.*

Kitty, who for the last two years had been sailing around Australia
with him, had just told him to *Piss Off.* And that was what he was
going to do.

He swiped his electronic key against the lock at the gates that led
down to F Finger, where his twenty-eight foot yacht, Intrepid, was berthed
amongst other, much bigger and more expensive yachts and catamarans.

It was a quarter past midnight. The tide was full. When he reached
Intrepid he untied the mooring lines, then jumped aboard and pulled

his little yacht out of its berth, using the stern line. He felt bad about not paying for his berth, but Kitty could attend to that. It was about time she paid for something.

Once free of the marina, he pulled up the mainsail, and flung the boom to starboard. He watched it fill. No one knew he was leaving. With a light south-easterly behind him, he followed the breakwater wall and slipped silently out of the harbour.

An hour later Kitty made her way slowly, very slowly, towards the marina. She was drunk. The path seemed to twist and tilt, as if it were alive, and she felt seasick. She bumped into a palm tree.

"Fuck you, Tug," she shouted into the night, bracing herself against the tree. "Fuck you and fuck Intrepid."

At the gate, her stupid electronic key didn't seem to connect and the gate refused to open. After a few moments she made her way to the amenities block.

Once out of the harbour, Tug unfurled the foresail on the port side, as the wind was behind him. He'd *wing and wing* it. Intrepid breasted the waves like Superman – arms flung wide. They were flying.

The sea came from behind. Every wave ran under the boat from stern to bow and the deck felt like a surfboard, lifting on the crests and plunging into the troughs.

Above, the sky was clear and moon-bright. Intrepid was a splinter on the ocean's skin. Tug knew this was where he belonged, and he didn't need Kitty and her harebrained schemes of regular jobs and settling down and having babies. Adventure called.

He pushed the autopilot button and sat back in the cockpit, listening to the shu-shushing of the waves against the bow, thanking GPS for guiding his boat. He blew a kiss up to the mighty sky. Somewhere up there, satellites beamed their positions to earth. It allowed him to take his hands off the tiller and trim the sails or check his charts, take a piss over the side or just lie back and relax. He didn't need Kitty.

He made his way down the companionway steps and over to the dinette table, where he had spread out the Whitsundays chart. He'd heard about Goldsmith Island – a good anchorage in a south-easterly, and he was busy measuring the distance between the current GPS position and Goldsmith, when he heard someone crying in the rear bunk.

At first he thought he was imagining it. Nights like this, the mind can play tricks. Nights like this he'd swear he'd seen ghosts leap out of the ocean and run along the sides of the boat, teasing and heckling. Then he heard it again.

He flicked on his torch and shone it on the bunk, where Kitty had dumped a bag of clothes from the laundromat. The bag was moving, and some of the laundry was escaping: her knickers and bras, a pair of shorts half in and half out of the drawstring opening. He pulled it open, and shook out their big beach towel, a couple of t-shirts and a bundle of white fur with eyes and ears and a voice: a white kitten.

"Shit!" He scooped it up in his hands. "Where the hell did you come from?"

But he knew the answer: the marina laundromat.

It's a custom amongst cruising boats to use marina laundromats for swapping books, magazines, old clothes, kitchen utensils and food – as well as gossip. The sign at the marina laundromat said: *Please place any unwanted goods on this shelf.* Kitty had taken an old muffin pan and some women's magazines up there this morning.

Tug stroked the kitten's head and it began to purr. He placed it on the galley bench, but it was unsteady on its feet and slid into the empty sink.

'She doesn't understand,' he explained to the kitten, as he poured some milk into a bowl and placed it too in the sink. 'We can't have a kid — not while we're sailing around Australia. She knows I've wanted to do this all my life. And I'd make a lousy father. I need my freedom!'

Kitty only just made it, diving into a cubicle and vomiting her heart out. Afterwards, she splashed water on her face and stared at her reflection in the mirror. Her mum would have said she looked like something the cat dragged in. She'd be right too! When her mum had met Tug she hadn't exactly been impressed.

She stroked her flat, empty abdomen — well, maybe not empty. Maybe there was a kid in there, feeding on her alcohol-laced blood. The kid'll be a retard. She'd have to get an abortion and Tug'd just have to pay for it, whatever it cost, because she'd just used up her last few dollars on the slot machines.

Tug was right, she *was* a stupid bitch. Stupid for forgetting to take her pill, stupid for going with Tug on this fantastical round-Australia voyage, stupid for running away from home, stupid for not finishing school.

She was sobbing as she left the toilets and made her way towards F Finger. She'd suddenly remembered the kitten that woman had given her in the laundromat. Poor little thing would be suffocating in that laundry bag. What sort of mother would she be if she couldn't even look after a kitten?

Meanwhile, Intrepid sailed just out of reach of one of three global positioning satellites. The autopilot beeped a warning and the rudder turned the boat 180 degrees to starboard. The boom jibed and the boat shuddered.

Tug had been dozing below decks, with the kitten purring in the crook of his arm. He leapt to his feet, dropped the kitten in the sink again, and climbed the steps to the cockpit.

It took a moment for him to work out what was happening. He swore at the autopilot, then ducked as the boom swung back again. It missed his head. He tugged on the mainsheet, locked it into position on the winch and then grabbed the tiller – pushing it to return to the course he'd originally set.

At the bow the foresail was flapping wildly, its sheets tying themselves together. He'd managed to reduce the swinging of the boom but he was going to have to go forward to untangle the sheets. He pressed the autopilot button again, and relaxed a little when it responded. It must have found what it was looking for.

Intrepid lurched drunkenly, port and starboard, as he made his way forward.

He reached for the lifelines that formed a wire fence around the edges of the deck, and then remembered – too late – that he hadn't fastened the 'gate' since leaving Curlew Sands. That was Kitty's job. He fell through. Saw black – above, below, all around him. Swallowed a gutful of salt water. It wasn't until he surfaced that he realised he'd fallen overboard. And there was no one on board, except a little white kitten – no one to throw him a life buoy.

On the pontoon next to the empty berth F28, Kitty looked into the black water. It was like a nightmare she used to have when she was a kid – that she'd come home from school and the ground had swallowed up her home. She expected to see a submerged Intrepid.

She checked the number on the pole next to the berth: F28, and it was the only empty one.

Her head began to spin, the pontoon was lurching and she fell to her knees, holding on tight, to save herself from falling into that black water.

Tug watched Intrepid shrink as it headed for the horizon. Another thing he'd forgotten when he left the marina was his inflatable life jacket. It was a golden rule on Intrepid. Kitty would complain, saying the weight of it hurt her neck, but he insisted.

He'd never be able to swim to safety and he wondered how long it would take, and how painful it would be, to drown. Maybe he'd be taken by a shark. At least that would make a quicker ending.

Then he saw fins coming towards him. Not sharks but dolphins.

Kitty loved the dolphins. They'd come every morning and evening with the sun, and they'd swim alongside the boat, riding the bow wave, sometimes rolling over, showing off their white bellies, leaping over the waves. Now he saw these slippery, shiny, sleek creatures gliding towards him. They circled. He could feel one beneath him, brushing his bare feet. Another bumped into his back — not roughly, a gentle push. And another brushed under his left arm, lifting it out of the water, then swimming around him again and lifting the other.

They want me to swim, he thought. And so he did, a slow overarm. And one dolphin swam beneath him, periodically rising, buoying him up. He could hear them now, chattering amongst themselves as they swam beside him, pushing and bumping him whenever he grew tired, urging him on, towards Intrepid.

Tug thought he may be dreaming, but maybe not. There'd been a story recently in the Curlew Sands News about a pod of dolphins herding a group of surfers away from a shark. Yachties' tales. He'd been known to tell some himself.

As he swam the horizon gave birth to a molten ball so bright it stung his eyes. Tug wanted to stop and watch the sunrise, but the dolphins scolded and pushed a little harder. His fingers were swollen, the skin white and wrinkled. He swallowed some water and coughed. It stung his throat and it was getting colder. How long does it take before hypothermia sets in?

Was Kitty also watching this magical sunrise? Sometimes she'd sit cross-legged on the deck and hum a single note as it rose. It was like a prayer, and when it had risen she'd turn towards him, that dreamy look in her eyes, and tell him everything was going to be okay now. He called it bullshit, but she really believed this stuff. Now it didn't seem such a good idea to leave her alone in Curlew Sands.

The wind had eased and the sails on Intrepid were hanging limp, moving side to side as the boat rocked gently with the sea. At last he was at the hull. Knotted sheets from the foresail were draped over the side. He grabbed them and pulled himself back onto the deck, where he collapsed, exhausted.

The sun warmed him and sleep beckoned until he heard dolphins bumping the hull. "Thank you," he called, as they swam towards the horizon.

Below, the kitten was still in the sink, waiting.

Kitty woke up, rubbing her eyes, as Intrepid nudged into berth F28.

"Grab the line, will you?" Tug threw the bowline at her.

She caught it and scrambled to her feet, then looped it, in figure-eights, around the cleat on the pontoon.

Tug cut the engine and lassoed another cleat with his stern line.

Kitty watched, hands on her hips. "Fuck you, Tug." The words exploded from her mouth. "Why'd you fuckin' leave me?"

Tug jumped down onto the pontoon and busied himself adjusting the lines. She wasn't going to help him anymore. Her head was pounding and she felt sick. His hair and beard were crusted with white and he was shivering.

"Shit! Look at you!" she squealed. "You're all salty."

"Went for a bit of a swim, that's all," he mumbled, tightening the springing line.

"You're an idiot, you know that?" She'd had enough of his bullshit stories.

He climbed back onto the boat and offered her his hand to pull her on board.

She didn't need it. She pulled herself up and they stood together in the cockpit for a moment, just facing each other. Then she sat down hard on the cockpit bench.

He sat opposite her, and took her hands in his, looking into her eyes. "I'm sorry," he said.

The kitten miaowed from the galley. Kitty pulled her hands away from him and climbed down the steps. Holding the kitten in front of her face she looked into its blue eyes. "And did you steer the boat while Tug was having a swim, then?" she asked.

"It was weird, that's all," said Tug from the cockpit.

"Yeah, well, I really don't care, do I?" she asked the kitten.

"I fell overboard," Tug began, "and these dolphins came and ..."

"I bet you're hungry," she said to the kitten. She opened a locker and moved tins of food around, with the kitten tucked under her arm. "I know. I bet you'd love some sardines ..."

"... and they rescued me." Tug followed her down the steps.

Kitty opened the can and scraped the sardines into the bowl that Tug had used for the milk.

She turned when he touched her on the shoulder and looked up at this man who was built like a tugboat, who was suddenly blocking the light from the companionway. 'You're dripping salt all over the boat, but what do I care?" She sniffed, and wiped fresh tears from her face with a tea towel. "It's your boat. You can fuckin' clean it up yourself!" She threw the tea towel at him and made for the rear bunk. "I'm outta here. I'm gonna ring mum and tell her I'm comin' home. You don't need me."

Tug brushed salt from his forearms into the galley sink while she flitted from one part of the boat to another, opening lockers, dragging things out, pushing them into her backpack.

"You got any money?" he asked.

That stopped her.

"How're ya gonna get home then?"

"Mum'll send me some money." She continued packing. The bag was already overflowing.

"I came back for you, Kitty. If it wasn't for the dolphins I wouldn't be here."

He wanted her to look at him, but she kept her head down. Now she was pulling things out of the bag and putting them back in the lockers. Did that mean she'd changed her mind?

"Don't leave me, Kitty. I need you. I really do." He said what he thought she wanted to hear.

She fastened the bag and slung it over her shoulder, then bent down to scoop up the kitten. "Here." She thrust it at him and climbed up onto the deck.

"Wait," Tug called. He dropped the kitten and followed her. "Wait." But she didn't stop. She didn't even turn around.

Tug hesitated. Dived down the companionway, then came up again. She was halfway along the F finger when he caught up to her. He grabbed her shoulder and pulled her back and she cowered. Did she really think he was going to hit her?

"You'll need this." He thrust a hundred dollar note into her hand, turned abruptly and walked back to Intrepid.

ALLISON MITCHELL *lives in Tasmania where she has spent most of her life. She's inspired to write by family stories of the past and events of the present. She was a finalist in the Tasmanian Writers' Prize in 2018 and is working on a novel based on life in the 1950s in the state's rugged west coast.*

Snake Gully

ALLISON MITCHELL

The steamship lurches away from the port. You stand on the deck and turn your back on Burnie. You turn your back on your parents, your home, Tasmania. Baby Charlotte is warm against you, her little body held to your chest, wrapped in your mother's old shawl. Her tiny face looks happy and that's how you feel. Jim walks away. You've seen his eyes and their sheen of tears and maybe he noticed your too-smug smile. In time, he'll realise this move is for the best. The work you've lined up for him in Bendigo is safe and will lead to a better life.

Young Peter follows in his father's wake and other passengers fill the space in a throng of brown and grey overcoats and felt hats. You sense the heightened emotions around you: anticipation, sorrow, excitement, fear. It's only you who laughs out loud at the freedom billowing from the ship's funnels, each puff of black smoke putting distance between you and Rosebery. You don't crane your neck for a last view of land, you look ahead at the open sea.

Alice tugs at your sleeve. "Can I go up there? There are too many people down here and I can't see." She points to the upper deck and walks towards the staircase.

"Stay here. That area's for the first-class passengers."

Alice frowns. She likes to argue, and since the accident, she's been worse. "But I can't see Grandmother and Aunt Edie. We promised we'd wave until we can't see each other anymore."

"Edie hasn't time for you," you tell her. "She's got to get your grandparents back to Rosebery."

You know they will still be standing there – Mother sobbing noisily into her best hanky and blaming Jim, her hopeless, hapless son-in-law, for taking you all away, Father regretting giving Jim five pounds in a rush of uncustomary generosity, and Edie resenting you for taking her beloved brother away.

"I could go and check."

You roll your eyes and breathe through gritted teeth, "That deck, up there, is reserved for those with money to waste on travelling first class, and you can't go up there."

"But I have a new dress and a new ribbon. I could pretend to be someone else's girl." Alice pats the ribbon in her hair.

"For goodness' sake, child. Your dress is new to you, but at least three of your cousins have worn it." Alice sets her jaw and stares up longingly. A man appears at the railing and looks down on you, his grey fedora tilted at the perfect angle. Then a woman peers over. There's a feather in her hat and her coat is straight from the fashion pages of the *Women's Weekly*, shapely and stylish with wide lapels. She obviously hasn't sat up 'till all hours squinting in the kerosene light, stabbing her fingers with pins, stitching heavy fabric, being interrupted by a crying baby, a child who has wet the bed and a husband dreaming he is choking on a pile of dirt.

A girl similar in age to Alice joins the couple on the upper deck.

"Mum, look! There's a girl. She has two ribbons. Look how wide they are." Alice waves to the girl, forgetting her fourth-hand dress, ignorant of the social miles between them. The girl waves back.

You return the same wooden smile her parents give you and tap Alice's shoulder. "See the difference? Her mother has a smart feathered cloche; I have a hat that your brother sat on and Charlotte's chewed. Now, go check Peter is alright and that Dad is minding him."

Alice watches the family disappear from the upper railing. She glares at you.

You glare back. "Go on, now."

After she's gone, you jig the baby onto your hip. With your free hand, you take your hankie from your pocket and dab at the trail of baby spit on your collar. The crowd disperses and you see Jim chatting to a man you haven't seen before. Alice is there and Peter is behind them, playing with a length of rope tied around a bollard.

It's not surprising Jim has found someone to speak to. He's good at making friends, winning people over — just lacks the guile to make a living from it. Thankfully, there'll be fewer people where you're going and no pub close by. He'll not be drinking after his shift 'till all hours nor walking down the town to do quick jobs for his family and friends — jobs that pay only in beer and a reason not to come home. You'll no longer be wondering if you should add water to the stew that's drying out on the stove or if you should be worrying about what's keeping him late. You smile at this thought.

Jim spots you and waves, pleased. He thinks your smile is for him. He moves himself between you and the breeze and puts his hand on your shoulder.

"Hey, Winsome. This is Mr Lowe. He used to work in Bendigo."

Mr Lowe nods at you. "You'll feel at home in Bendigo, Mrs Hogan, with the clatter of the mine. It's right in town, just like it is in Rosebery."

"Oh, we won't be in town," you say. "Jim has decided to be a farmer, working with my brother." You credit Jim with the move. You say he's working with your brother, not for him. Once Jim knows what's what, you'll get your own farm—you'll see to that.

Mr Lowe has a pack of cigarettes and taps it on his palm. "Sea's calm this trip," he says. "Not like my last one. Couldn't keep a beer down the waves were that rough."

Alice's eyes widen. "How big were they?"

"It wasn't the size. It was that they kept coming and the wind was something fierce. All the way from Burnie, until we got this side of the Rip. I felt for those blokes shovelling the coal into the furnace down below. Tough buggers, but they got shook up pretty bad and had to be carried off when we docked in Melbourne."

Jim shivers. He doesn't normally feel the cold. "You wouldn't catch me down there feeding the fire." He doesn't normally smoke either, but he takes the cigarette Mr Lowe offers.

"I don't blame you, cobber. You were in that accident, weren't you?" says Mr Lowe. "I hear they've moved Ivan Petrenko and his missus out of the company houses down to one of those shacks in Snake Gully. He's no use to the mine anymore."

Peter stops playing with the rope, pulls his left arm into his body, tilts his head to one side and limps. "Mr Petrenko walks like this now," he says. He has one eye shut tight and lets his tongue hang from his mouth, making his expression grotesque.

"Stop that, Peter." Your tone is sharp. Jim needs no reminders if he is to sleep at night. Peter winces and takes your hand, not sure what he's done.

Mr Lowe lights Jim's cigarette. "Sounds crook. What happened down there?"

...

You don't want to remember that day, but you can't help it. You remember being pleased the washing was dry. You remember taking it off the line at the same time as wondering how many rounds Jim had had at the pub to make him late. It'll serve him right if his tea is tough and tasteless, you were thinking.

Alice came running into the yard, saying something was wrong at the mine. Charlotte was due and kicking, but you still managed to drag Peter down the hill to the work site. Alice ran by your side, saying that the problem was in the mining section and the afternoon shift was still down there.

Jim's section, Jim's shift.

You remember being at the mine's entrance. Managers, workers, wives, family, neighbours, all gathered, waiting for news. It was only the currawongs stopping things from being deathly quiet, a great mob of them filling the air with their loud, discordant shrieks. Then, they fell silent too when Jim came out of the shaft, staggering under the weight of Mr Petrenko.

You saw the men running to lift Mr Petrenko from Jim. Doris Petrenko running too, her grey hair trailing from her usually neat bun. Alice hugging her father and you following, but the blood and dirt on Jim's face stopped you. If he was hurt, you wouldn't cope. It was no good here. You had to get away. In your head you'd already written another letter to your brother in Bendigo, begging him to help.

. . .

Early morning light shines through the porthole and you feel the ship's gentle motion. You're cuddled up to Charlotte and whisper in her ear, "We're on our way to a new life. Things will be different now. Daddy will be home safe and on time every night." Charlotte gurgles. You're lighter than you have felt in ages, and it must show on your face because Jim looks at you like he used to. You sweep a curl of hair behind your ear and a wisp of happiness floats between you. He and Alice and Peter go out on deck, and you give Charlotte another feed before you follow them. Jim and Peter stand at the ship's bow.

"Where's Alice?" you ask.

Jim's face tenses. He sees you're cross. "Alice can take care of herself. She's probably gone to find that other girl."

"She can't simply run about the ship. She's too wilful and you're a pushover. You'll have to discipline her. My father would have taken the belt to me if I gadded about the way Alice does." Your voice is shrill.

Jim flinches. "Our daughter watched me drag a man from the mine. She ran to me and held me, never mind the dirt and blood." He looks down and quietly hisses at your boots. "Come on, Winnie, let her have some fun."

He's soft, smothered by his family, and Edie in particular. That's why you take care of things. There's a chatter of girlish voices from above. Of course, it's Alice on the upper deck with her posh friend.

Alice must see your fury but she ignores it. "Hello," she shouts. "This is my friend, Jacqueline. She's going to be a flower girl at her brother's wedding." Jaqueline waves.

"Come down this instant," you shout. The ship rocks and you wobble. Alice laughs and dances around with the other girl, moving with the sea's motion.

Peter looks green. "I don't feel well." You take his hand.

"Get down here, now, Alice!" Jim shouts. He never shouts. He races past you towards the stern and up the staircase to the girls. Over the bow, you see a wave, smooth and even, like a big high-topped loaf coming towards you. You move your feet apart and grasp Peter to you and you both stay upright, riding the ship up and over the wave.

"Hold on to the rail." Jim's sharp, not like you've ever heard him before. He's with Alice on the stairs and he's holding her tight. You wedge Peter between you and the rail. The next wave is larger and the one behind that larger still. You don't want to be there, but you're too scared to move. The first wave rolls under the rear of the ship, lifts a sharp angle and with more force. And when the next one comes, it's all you can do to stay on your feet. The ship takes you over. That might be the end of it.

Then the ship falls.

You lose your balance and lean heavily on Peter. He cries out. Fear has you in its vicious grip.

Mr Lowe pulls you up, then helps Peter. "It's breakfast time. Let's get you back to your room." He is reassuring and you breathe easier. He carefully pries Peter's hand from the rail and places it in your hand. Peter doesn't complain that your hold is too tight.

Mr Lowe sees you've frozen where you stand. "Go to the cabin," he says. You've gone a few feet when the next wave knocks you over and Peter lands next to you. You hear Jim tell Mr Lowe to help others. Jim's back on your deck and he has Alice. He pulls you up and pushes you on and does the same with the children.

"Run! Wave … a giant wave! Run. Run. Run." It's a frantic yell from someone, somewhere, but you're already running. You lose your balance and fall. You look back. The wave is huge, a monster, higher than the upper deck, higher than Mount Black. Terrifying in size; sharp and foaming on its silent, relentless course towards the ship. Jim manages you all, carrying, dragging, shoving, urging you on. Your heart beats loud above the chaos.

Demons play with the ship, lift it from the end, slam its nose down, shaking people loose. Hard, sharp, objects slide fast and treacherous from the back of the ship, bashing your legs. Jim holds back what he can and then keeps you from joining the violent slip, slide and ricochet down the deck.

You can't see Alice, but her screams let you know she's still there. You drag Peter a few more steps to an open cabin door and shove him inside. A box rocks against your legs and knocks you away before you can follow him. A towering wave falls on you in a thunder of ice-blue water. It smashes you into the rail and then back against the cabin wall. Next, you roll past the open cabin that might have saved you. In terror, you grab at a dark shadow. It's Jim's coat. It's pulled from your grasp and Jim and his coat sweep out of sight, part of the fast-moving torrent.

You're like a twig in swift and towering rapids. You can't think. You can't feel. You can only grab at anything to get your head above water to air. But there is no air, only freezing, overflowing, suffocating water. You crash against the rail again, catch it and cling on. Others, skittled by the water's force, shoot past to goodness knows where.

Then the ship rights itself. The demons rest. Flows reverse and drain back into the sea, allowing you great gulping noisy breaths of air. Jim wades over with Alice. You pull her into your arms and collapse together amid the turmoil.

"You're doing champion," says Jim. The words wheeze from him between his own deep breaths. You want to shake the water out of yourself and him and Alice. But there's no time. The bow of the ship dips again, into the giant valley between giant waves. "Nooo," Alice shouts.

Jim grabs the belt from Alice's coat and ties it around her and the rail. "Hold on girls, just hold on. You can do it, you can." He takes the belt of his trousers and straps you in the same way.

"Not again." Alice shakes her head. You're the same—you can't do it again. The blood in your veins is like lightning, making your heart work too hard and your head throb.

"One more time, darling girls. We'll get out of this. Soon. Just hold on." Then Jim's legs go from under him, and he's rushed along with everything else that's not tied down.

"Jim, come back," you yell. The bow drops, then the ship rolls to one side, almost dipping you into the sea. Shadows like sacks fall from above you and into the ocean. There's no time to draw breath before water floods over you. The ship rolls and you glimpse a face in the sea. It's Alice's friend. Her eyes wide, terrified. One envied ribbon trails behind her, the other gone. The girl reaches out, but you're too far away, held firmly by Jim's belt. You choke on water and horror, and hope Alice didn't see.

The ship rights itself. The sea drains back to where it came from. Alice coughs water down her chin. You reach for her and take her icy hand in yours. She manages a limp, trembling squeeze, but neither of you try to untangle yourselves from the rail.

The sea calms and the ship turns. "We'll wait for your father."

Finally, it's Mr Lowe, not Jim, who unties you and sets you free.

Heavy, wet sobs break out of Alice. "Where's Dad?"

Mr Lowe pulls you up and sets you steady. "Your baby's safe Mrs Hogan. Your boy too." He lifts Alice and carries her towards the cabins.

"Where's Jim." He doesn't answer. You stumble after him and catch his sleeve. "Where's my husband?"

Mr Lowe looks over the stern and you follow his glance. Jim's on the deck, lying with his head hard against the bollard that Pete had been playing round. You run over and kneel at his side before the bloody gash on his forehead stops you. A moment later, you gently take his head onto your lap.

"Mum, is Dad sleeping? Is he sleeping?" Alice is desperate, like you. "His eyes are shut, like Mr Petrenko. Is he going to be crippled like Mr Petrenko?"

Mr Lowe holds her, steps around Jim and carries her away. You can't give her any comfort. Other voices vaguely penetrate your numbed mind.

"The Captain's taken the ship back out to calmer water."

"That was some set of waves."

"What a freak."

"That family that was going to the wedding's missing. Likely gone overboard."

You stroke Jim's lifeless face. Your brother won't want you now. Not without Jim. You're no use to him and will have to return to Rosebery. You will be no use there either, not to the mining company, nor your family and you'll be expected to be grateful for a damp old shack next to the Petrenkos in Snake Gully.

TERRY MULHERN is a writer who splits his time between Somerset in northwest Tasmania and Melbourne, Victoria. Terry's writing spans themes of Tasmanian history, ecology, and culture.
Terry won the 2020-21 Van Diemen History Prize with his essay "Insubordination and Improper Intimacy". His 2018-19 entry, "St Valentine's Tears" was highly commended. He has also published in Forty South Tasmania, Science Write Now, Pursuit *and the* Papers and Proceedings of the Royal Society of Tasmania.
His short story "The Satchel" was a finalist in the 2021 Tasmanian Writer's Prize and appears in the Forty South Short Story Anthology 2021.
For more of Terry's writing see www.terrymulhern.com
Born in north Queensland, Terry has worked at universities in the UK and around Australia, but he only feels truly at home in the northwest of Tasmania.

The flying fish

TERRY MULHERN

DECEMBER 1833, LONDON

The morning post was waiting for Mary Grimstone when she sat down to breakfast. Eagerly, she picked up the fat envelope from Van Diemen's Land. Her sister had outdone herself, she thought, sending so much news. But as Mary started to read, her face fell.

My dearest Mary,
Knowing how fond you became of Mr. Hellyer, that most pleasing and considerate of
travelling companions, I know that your heart will be torn asunder by the melancholy
news I must now relate . . .

· · ·

The smiling first officer passed Henry Hellyer the flying fish. As Henry grasped it about its middle, it extended its wings and vigorously flipped-flopped its body.

"Oh, my word!" said Henry, almost dropping the wriggling, slippery fish. Both Mary and Henry laughed.

Bearing the iridescent, glistening creature in his hands, Henry rushed below deck to his cabin. Delicately, he laid the flying fish on the table. Its gills opened and closed ever more slowly. The fish's colours, so vivid in the early morning light, darkened before his eyes as its life ebbed away. Working quickly with pencil and ink, Henry rendered the shape of its slender body, the upward sweep of its wings and the sharp angles of its tail. With a brush, he added colour. First, a pink wash on its belly, then green and blue above. With a fine brush licked to a point, he picked out each scale with dark pigment. With tiny radiating strokes, Henry faded the tint outwards, more than one hundred times. Row upon row of scales with their dark centres aligning along its flank.

Henry was pleased with how he'd captured the way light played upon the translucent scales. Later, when the watercolour was dry, he pasted it into his journal facing the day's entry — *Novr 3rd 1825*.

· · ·

A loud grinding crunch startled Henry. He spun around and watched a massive boulder bound down the mountainside. Eventually, the huge, bouncing, spinning stone disappeared with a thrashing crash into the eucalypt forest lapping at the mountain's lower slopes.

Turning to the two men under his command, Isaac Cutts and Richard Fredricks, Henry demanded,

"Why did you do that?"

"It moved when I put me foot on it," said Fredricks, "it deserved it for scarin' me."

"Well, enough tomfoolery," said Henry, "assist me in placing this marker at the very peak."

For posterity, Henry had carved a message into the thick trunk of a stunted tree, blown over below the summit.

St. Valentine's Peak

14 Feb '27

H. H.

VDL Co.

They lugged the heavy timber up the vast pile of boulders to the highest point and wedged it among the huge grey stones.

Pulling out his compass and notebook, Henry meticulously took bearings to distant landforms. With his surveyor's duties done, he called Fredricks and Cutts to re-join him. With open bible in hand, Henry cleared his throat.

"And the LORD said unto Abram. Lift up now thine eyes, and look from the place where thou art northward, and southward, and eastward, and westward: for all the land which thou seest, to thee will I give it, and to thy seed for ever. Arise, walk through the land in the length of it and in the breadth of it; for I will give it unto thee."

Fredricks nudged Cutts and smirked at the mention of "seed". Lost in exhilaration, Henry didn't notice. Below, to the south and west, lay more than fifty square miles of rolling grassland.

The next day, the wind got up as they marched across the plain. Pale rippling waves chased each other across the golden sea of grass. In the afternoon, they entered a patch of blackened country. But among the scorched tussocks, fresh green shoots proliferated.

"Fredricks, how do you think this fire started?" asked Henry.

"I seen lightnin' start fires in the bush in New South Wales," replied Fredricks.

Cutts chimed in, "Maybe the blacks lit it to flush out game?"

"Yes, I suppose they might've," said Henry, considering another possibility.

"At home," said Henry, "farmers fire the moorland to remove gorse and refresh the pasture. Are the natives capable of such practices?"

"Nah," said Fredricks dismissively, "'round Sydney, I've never seen the blacks do nowt but drink grog and sit 'round waitin' for rations and blankets to be doled out."

As they progressed, Henry was struck by how elegantly the gently undulating plain was decorated with small glades of blackwoods, separated by hundreds of acres of grass. They crossed crystal-clear brooks dancing over pebbly bottoms. It reminded Henry of the grand parkland he'd once visited, expertly designed for Viscount Palmerston by the great Capability Brown.

With each step, weight lifted from Henry's shoulders. The frustrating months of pushing through wet forests full of tangled horizontal scrub and climbing range after range of mountains were over. He would cut a road from Emu Bay, thirty miles to the north, and the company's indentured servants and flocks of sheep would come. At last, he could begin his true task and not simply be a footsore explorer and surveyor.

In his mind's eye, Henry could see it all. Where he'd place whitewashed cottages for the company's workers and their families. The church, built from local stone, with its belltower poking above encircling myrtles. Flocks grazing in perfectly geometric fields enclosed by wattle and bauera hedgerows. Gentlefolk on horseback trotting along eucalypt-shaded, arrow-straight lanes. This is how he would be remembered – the famed architect of a new model agrarian society.

The following day, the grassland gradually gave way to lightly wooded country as they neared the forested mountains at the western edge of the plain. Unexpectedly, they came upon a cluster of bark huts by the side of a creek. Fredricks and Cutts unslung their muskets and cocked them.

"Halloooo," called Henry in a cheery voice.

There was no response.

"It appears nobody's home," said Henry, as he leant down and peered into the low opening of the largest hut. He took off his pack and crawled in.

"I imagine a dozen natives could sleep in here!" shouted Henry to Fredricks and Cutts, who remained outside, still on edge.

As his eyes grew accustomed to the dimness, Henry saw the walls were decorated with charcoal drawings. One showed the crescent moon above men and animals. With his knife, Henry cut away the sheet of bark. Then he crawled back out.

"Look at this – there's an artist among them!" said Henry enthusiastically, showing Fredrick and Cutts the drawing. They were nonplussed.

"I think we best be movin' on, Mr Hellyer," said Fredricks, "it wouldn't be wise to wait here for the savages to come back 'ome. I don't think they'd take too kindly to you nickin' that picture off their parlour wall."

"When I was last in Launceston," added Cutts, "Mr. Gibson's men from the Western Marshes told me they often need to drop four or five crows, just to keep the peace, like."

Aghast, Henry recoiled and countered, "Before I departed England, I discussed the topic of the natives with the company directors. We agreed to endeavour to raise them from their state of precarious subsistence to one of material comfort and spiritual fulfilment as Christian herdsmen, labourers and domestic servants for the company."

"Aye, Mr. Hellyer," said Fredricks, who turned away so Henry would not see the look of disbelief on his face.

. . .

Hobart's weak autumn sun shone in the sitting room window. After replacing her teacup, Mary lifted the *Colonial Advocate* from the tray. As she settled herself to read, something at the bottom of the front page caught her eye. *Female Writer, Extract of a letter from a Lady Residing in Hobart Town, Van Diemen's Land, inserted from the London Morning Herald.* Her heart stopped.

"Oh, dear God," exclaimed Mary.

Meanwhile, in government house, Colonel Arthur bellowed for Colonial Secretary Burnett.

"Yes, your excellency?" enquired Burnett timorously.

"Have you read the *Colonial Advocate* this morning?" returned Arthur, "No? Well, let me." Arthur read aloud.

"'You could hardly imagine that a country like England could produce such an illiterate cub as this colony. Saturn is not more remote from the Sun, than Hobart Town from all science and literature.'"

Looking up, Arthur said, "And don't worry, it gets better. 'The government and law officers, etc., form, and are completely the aristocracy. They are dull, reserved, punctiliously jealous of compromising their rank, all etiquette and caution. One reason for all this is that there are a great many mushrooms amongst them; and there is no pride so stiff and ungraceful as upstarts.'"

Burnett thought to himself the "mushroom" analogy was rather perceptive.

"Oh, and here's the best part," seethed Arthur. "'Entertainments are occasionally given; but, as Madame de Stael says of the Germans, they are rather ceremonies than parties of pleasure; and this remark applies to,'" here Arthur placed emphasis, "'*the first house in this place*. A card for a dinner party gives me the horrors. Often, very often, I had much rather stay at home; but, like the poor king of Arragon, "etiquette won't let me."'"

Arthur paused.

"Does she think I host her here because I enjoy her scintillating conversation? It is *etiquette* that forces me to extend invitations to her! Burnett, this will not do," hissed Arthur, "Who does she think she is? She is nothing and nobody here. The widowed sister-in-law of a pompous fool in the employ of a failing company of dubious motive and action! I only tolerate the impertinence of their agent, that Catholic upstart Curr, because so many damned MPs are shareholders, or sit on the company's court of directors." Arthur stomped over to the window and stared out upon a rain sodden Davey Street. "Furthermore, Mrs Grimstone's novel is feminine melodramatic nonsense."

"Yes, sir," said Burnett, "indeed." And then quizzically, regretting the question before it left his lips, "you've read it, sir?"

"Of course, I haven't!" barked Arthur, 'What do you take me for? As if I have time for reading such twaddle.'

Burnett shuffled his feet. "It's only that Mrs Burnett is keen to get her hands on a copy ..."

"Tell her to talk to my wife," said Arthur, "but mark my words Burnett, Mrs Grimstone shall feel no small discomfiture for this insult. Strike her name from the guest lists for all upcoming events at Government House. If she despises Hobart society so, then her wish to stay home is granted. She no longer exists. And anyone who thinks otherwise will receive the same treatment."

A smile formed on Arthur's thin lips.

"I'll wager she'll be on a ship home in less than three months."

. . .

It was after midnight when Henry turned the final page and closed the report to the House of Commons *on the subject of the military operations lately carried on against the Aboriginal inhabitants of Van Diemen's Land*. He sat back, shaking his head. It contained barely a mention of the company and none of the things he told Colonel Arthur's conciliator to the natives, George Augustus Robinson.

Five-and-a-half years since he climbed St Valentine's Peak. Five-and-a-half years of unremitting extirpation of the local blacks by the company's men. And yet, not a word about any of it. The murders and massacres he'd listed. The names of stockkeepers who took women and girls as slaves. The poisoned flour. The hunting parties. The heads on spikes. Nothing.

Unsure if he was more appalled or relieved, Henry sat dumbfounded. He'd been anxious about what would happen when the truth came out – it would be obvious who was responsible. But there was nothing in the report. Nothing. Did Robinson even relate these events to Arthur? For the life of him, Henry couldn't work out what'd happened. Why would Robinson withhold the information? Maybe Robinson did report it and it was Arthur who chose not to tell the government in London? But why?

No wonder, thought Henry grimly, Mr Curr smiled like "the cat that got the cream" when he handed him the book that morning, saying, "Here you are Hellyer, I received this yesterday. You should read it ..."

A whitewash, mused Henry bitterly. So much blood, and yet no stains to show for it.

And now the vile whispering behind his back had started again. Was it meant to shut him up? And when it didn't, was it meant to discredit him when he arrived in Hobart to join the Survey Department? Henry felt sick. With Mary gone, he had no allies to defend his reputation.

Sliding open the bureau drawer, Henry looked down on the pistol and powder flask. Gingerly, he lifted the weapon and placed it next to the book. Tears rolled down Henry's cheeks as he dipped his pen and started to write. The scratching of the nib upon the paper seemed so very loud.

. . .

Mary read on.

> . . . Mr. Hellyer is dead, and I am deeply saddened to add that this was done by his own hand. I will not repeat here all the details of the affair, but instead have included copies of two letters. One received from Circular Head laying out the horror of the events and the other written by Mr. Hellyer the night he died (September 1st 1832). I know how deep your affection was for the poor man and you would not wish to be spared any detail, no matter how distressing. Each day I thank God you are still with us, having conquered your own demons of the mind. Alas, Mr. Hellyer did not possess your strength.
>
> God Bless you and keep you my beloved Mary,
>
> Your loving sister, Lucy

Mary put down Lucy's note. She unfolded the copy of Henry's letter. Inhaling deeply, she began to read. It took some time to get beyond the first line.

> I am asking myself this question, "what evil hath he done?"

In a state of shock, Mary climbed the stairs to her writing room. She rummaged through cupboards and boxes until she found what she was looking for. It reminded her of a happier time, many years ago, and a tropical sea bathed in warmth and light.

. . .

The sun slipped below the distant purple horizon and a warm breeze filled the sails. Henry and Mary walked sedately along the windward side of the main deck.

"Thank you, Mr Hellyer, for allowing me to borrow your journal," said Mary.

"My pleasure, Mrs Grimstone," replied Henry.

"I was struck by the beauty of your illustrations," said Mary, "I didn't realise you were so talented. Your flying fish, in particular, is quite beautiful."

"You are too kind," said Henry.

"It also helped order in my mind," said Mary, "the chain of events of that tumultuous week before we reached Rio. I was so shaken, I failed to make complete notes of it in my own diary."

"Indeed," said Henry, "the whole affair was rather singular. Our Captain revealed himself to be a man of exceptionally low character."

Lowering her voice, so any nearby crew wouldn't overhear, Mary said, "Yes, to attempt to seduce my maid would have been enough, but to then take up with Mrs Curr's maid and install her in his cabin as his mistress is quite obscene."

"And when confronted by Mr Curr," responded Henry, "to wave loaded pistols at him and accuse us all of plotting mutiny. Extraordinary!"

"Extraordinary," agreed Mary.

They walked on.

"I still struggle," said Mary, "to understand how the British Consul in Rio managed to conciliate Mr Curr and Captain Kellie."

"Ah," said Henry, "Mr Curr values the company's good name too much to allow the details of this tawdry affair to become known. To change ships would have required considerable explanation."

"Of course," added Henry, "Mr Curr has sworn me and the other company officers to secrecy."

With a twinkle in his eye, Henry glanced around, leaned close, and whispered, "But perhaps, a "Captain Kellie" might make a fine villain for your next novel. He is both dangerous and dashingly handsome. I often find myself all aquiver in his company."

"Oh, Mr Hellyer," laughed Mary, "you are wicked."

...

Reaching up, Mary pulled her scrapbook off the shelf. Carefully, she pasted the flying fish onto a fresh page. Staring at the watercolour, she pondered what she should write. Finally, the tears came in great heaving floods. When she was done, Mary picked up her pen and wrote.

> *This drawing was done for me by a friend and fellow passenger, Henry Hellyer Esqr. As we often sat or walked together on the deck, how little did he or I imagine the tragedy life would be to him. How well it is that the book of futurity is shut from us. Poor Hellyer! I have heard he committed suicide. I never heard anything that shocked me more. He ended all with a pistol. How many has slander slain! I who now write of him — sigh for him — what may be my own destiny. I am very low tonight.*
> *22 Dec.ʳ 1833. Sunday*

AUTHOR'S NOTE: This is a fictionalised account of real events.

Mary Leman Grimstone (née Rede) was an English poet and novelist who resided in Hobart 1826-29. Enroute to Hobart, Mary befriended Henry Hellyer, an officer in the Van Diemen's Land Company and colleague of her brother-in-law.

Henry's journal, "Voyage to Van Diemen's Land", is held by the Tasmanian Archives and Heritage Office. His description of his 1827 trek to St Valentine's Peak was published in the Company's 1832 Annual Report. Mary's letter to the London *Morning Herald* appeared in the *Colonial Advocate* on May 1, 1828. Her personal scrapbook is in Yale University's Beinecke Rare Book and Manuscript Library. In it are two watercolour sketches by Henry. It also contains Mary's account of the shipboard scandal, a letter describing Henry's death, and a transcript of his suicide note. The original was found atop an open copy of Lieutenant Governor Arthur's report to the House of Commons on the Black War.

SHARYN MUNRO *is an author, award-winning short-story writer, essayist, public speaker and "literary activist". Her three non-fiction books are* The Woman on the Mountain *(Exisle 2007),* Mountain Tails *(Exisle 2009), and* Rich Land, Wasteland *(Pan Macmillan/Exisle 2012). She lived alone for years in a solar-powered mudbrick cabin on her remote NSW mountain wildlife refuge, where her first two books were set. Now she lives on the NSW mid-north coast.*

She also writes freelance non-fiction articles, but her favourite genre is the short story, and hers have won many awards, including first prizes nationally as in the Alan Marshall Award and the Boroondara. She received the 2014 NSW Nature Conservation Council's Dunphy Award for "The most outstanding environmental effort of an individual". Her website, www.sharynmunro.com, houses her ongoing nature blog, background information, and her books, and she continues to have a large following on Facebook.

Shellgrit

SHARYN MUNRO

From the sea edge of her long rock platform, Rachel turned around to catch the sun's last brushes of old gold on the island's highest trees. This had been a low tide discovery, but that was hours ago; she ought to head back. Sunburnt and salt encrusted, she tied her towel around her waist.

Searching the darkening cliffs for a landmark to memorise the position of her find, she squinted; there seemed to be something pale … pink? … moving steadily along the top. It looked frothy, insubstantial; then a section of the pink froth detached itself and began making a beckoning gesture.

Rachel snapped to the realisation of how far out she was, with the sea already over her ankles, small waves creaming around the rocks. She concentrated on making her way past the hidden rock pools, alert for their chains of yellow ochre pods.

The incoming tide had spread alarmingly far up the sand by the time she reached there. Scanning the cliff for her apparition, she could only see treetop silhouettes against a bruised sky. The track up was barely visible; on top, it was clearly marked with crushed white shells, luminous in the dusk. There was no sign of her would-be rescuer.

She jogged along the path as quickly as she dared, her sandshoes squelching and scrunching with each step fall. Fruit bats squealed through the trees above; strange shapes loomed in the shadows. The track veered inland, down through the familiar glade of tall lemon-scented gums that told her the cabins were just over the hill. When the night hum of the generator reached her ears, for once she welcomed it.

As the path became the soft sand of the landward side of the island, she could see the lights of the house on the headland and the five cabins dotted through the trees on the edge of the lagoon. Their cabin's kerosene lamps were lit; Jo would have been back well before dusk from her fishing trip with some of their neighbours. Vegetarian Rachel didn't like watching anyone catch fish, so they had split up for the afternoon.

She hoped Jo had enjoyed herself, as she'd been expressing doubts about this island holiday – the cabins were tatty, fibro, "jerry built", as her father would say; "quaint", protested Rachel, for whom the experience of being on a real island was enough. Her awareness had remained acute, of being on a solitary lump of land in the middle of the sea, of its sense of restriction and yet of perfect totality.

They'd been escaping the heat in the airconditioned Rockhampton Post Office, writing a few postcards and debating where to go next. Overhearing them, a middle-aged, half-erased gentleman had introduced himself as "Armstrong" in a voice that was either posh or English. He'd said the islands were far better than the coast here, mentioning a cancellation, a cabin now available on an island an hour's boat ride away; inexpensive, casual, unspoilt. The price being incredibly low, they'd agreed to a week there.

Escorting them to a small fibro house in one of the town's wide streets to buy their tickets, he tossed a few muttered words through the back screen door, beckoned them in, and disappeared.

The "booking office" was the kitchen. At the table a big woman with starkly-hennaed hair sat, overflowing her floral shift, painting her fingernails. She'd thrown them one sharp blue look, and turned half her attention to business, the other half remaining with the five blood-red nails.

She informed them that the boat, the Shady Lady, was leaving from Yeppoon in two hours and they should bring all their own food and drink. Rachel handed her the money. One-handed, she wrote out their receipt, and as she handed it to them, Rachel could smell her sweat and stale perfume.

They'd rushed off to buy provisions before driving across to the harbour. Waiting for the boat to appear, they agreed it was smart to be getting out to an island. Reef-protected, the shore here was unattractive, the water flat and lukewarm.

When the Shady Lady had nosed up to the jetty, they'd been surprised to see the faded gentleman at the helm. More surprisingly, they learnt that the taciturn giantess was his wife. The island and the boat were owned by them, and his twin sister and her husband, who lived over there. The Armstrong children had apparently grown up on the island. Rachel was intrigued, wanting to know more of the story, but their skipper clearly intended to remain a closed book.

The island was casual all right. Although she was late tonight, Rachel needed a shower to ease her sunburn. Under the single dim light of the "amenities", she recalled their first tryout of the shower – roofless, with partial tin surrounds for modesty, rough cement slab underfoot. Jo's appalled reaction had not been soothed by the large green frogs which lurked there.

Rachel unhooked her top, breasts drooping coolly damp against the hot skin below; the gritty bikini bottom scraped her already tender thighs as she peeled it down. The bucket was already full of brackish water from the well, which always smelt vaguely of something dead. Lowering the canvas bag, she emptied the bucket into it, then hauled the bag back up and secured it. The water dripped lazily through the holes of the no-longer-adjustable rose, but it was refreshing. She left it dripping and the frogs croaking, wrapped her towel around herself and hurried up to the cabin.

"Hi Jo!" she called.

Jo spun around. "Oh, Rach, I was getting worried!"

"Yeah, sorry; got a bit worried myself. Stayed too long over the other side. Let's have a beer and I'll tell you about it; I'm parched."

Pulling on briefs and an oversize T-shirt, she joined Jo out front. Beers in hand, they flopped into canvas chairs facing the water and the twinkling mainland.

"The ocean side is something else, Jo; you wouldn't see a single light from there. I found a great rock platform, really long and thin, and I saw the weirdest thing … only I still don't know what it was … but it waved me in off the rocks 'cause the tide was coming in."

"What do you mean, 'thing'?"

"Well, I suppose it must have been a person, but it was a strange shape, or in a strange getup. The light was going, I couldn't see properly. Come for a walk with me tomorrow around sunset; we might see it again."

"Oh Rachel, you and your imagination! Anyway, we're going on that boat trip to the far reef tomorrow, remember?"

"Ah ... that's right. Well, maybe we'll be back in time. Anyway, here's to our third tropical day!"

"And night," added Jo, stretching to clink her beer on Rachel's. The movement lifted one small breast clear of her sarong.

"I'll drink to that," said Rachel.

Early next morning, they met the brother-in-law, Larry, when he came to fill the kero fridge and lamps. Burnt a dark reddish brown, glistening with sweat, he was clad only in faded navy shorts, above which loomed a massive beer belly and heavy boobs. Sharp light blue eyes gave him a predatory look. Incongruously, his wavy brown hair was oiled back like a matinée Romeo's.

In no hurry to leave, lounging against their doorway, he began telling them how each year he "made a packet" on a prawning boat up the Gulf.

"So who does your job here when you're prawning?" she asked. "Your wife?"

"Her! Nah, the missus is too delicate to handle garbage 'n' stuff; bit of a' invalid ... good for bloody nuthin'. Nah, Chuckie stops over 'ere during the season."

"Chuckie?"

"Charles," drawled Larry, "Lord Muck, me brother-in-law."

"Ah yes, your wife's family owned this island, I believe?" said Jo.

"Yeah. Useless lot they were. They done nuthin' with the place; said they liked it natural! There weren't no improvements at all, 'part from the house, till I came here in '58 … after the oldies'd drowned in that storm." He slapped the door jamb. "Yep, I built all these cabins meself. Dunno what that sappy pair would've done without me sister'n me."

"Your sister?" echoed Rachel.

"Yeah, Beryl. Dincha meet her when youse paid?"

"Oh … yes, we did," murmured Rachel, beginning to get a nasty taste in her mouth.

She got up to clear away the breakfast things; Larry took the hint. The girls moved to the back doorway to wave as he climbed into his old jeep.

"Oh my God! Look at his feet!" hissed Jo.

Rachel looked; they were no longer feet, they were broad thick pads of hard calloused dead flesh, greyish-white under the dirt, split with deep and wide ancient cracks all around.

"I feel sick," she said.

"Ugh! Imagine being in bed with that!" shuddered Jo. "He's enough to turn any girl lesbian," she giggled.

But Rachel wasn't listening; she was throwing up in the sink.

She could not go on the boat trip, but insisted Jo went anyway.

"Sunstroke," pronounced Jo.

"Suppose so," said Rachel, feeling it more a blow to her heart than her head. The cabins were no longer quaint; they were excrescences. "Larrybuilt", she thought sourly. How had the twins fallen into the clutches of this awful pair?

Too depressed to cope with her thoughts, she went back to bed. She slept until well after mid-day, waking hot and thirsty amidst damp and twisted sheets. Downing great draughts of water, she splashed more on her face, then wandered round to the southern point of the island in search of a cooling breeze.

She stretched out under a pandanus tree, soothed by the sea's constant rush on the smooth pebbles that floored this small cove. Her mind kept returning to the original Armstrong family of island dwellers, inventing histories for them … recluses, eccentrics, a skeleton in the Armstrong closet? Whatever, they must have had a private income.

This small island on the other side of the world was the perfect hideaway for a couple who needed no other company. They'd have had all they needed: books, music, painting, studying natural history, tropical sunsets, each other … and then the twins. What must it have been like for *them*, to grow up on an island?

It was difficult to imagine the reserved Charles even taking off his shoes; she could not see him as a boy running half-naked through the shallows. Would they have gone to boarding school? No, School of the Air, probably. But after that, what opportunities for romance? Hard to imagine kindred spirits in Yeppoon.

She could see the rhythm of their cultured island life simply continuing. Except they were no longer children. Rachel frowned; she'd read how close twins could be, and in this isolation extending that closeness must have been practically inevitable. Non-judgemental Rachel sighed with relief; so they may have been happy for a time. But why, oh why, these grotesque later pairings?

Perhaps they married for propriety's sake, or perhaps their parents, thinking them lonely — or knowing they weren't — had wanted to ensure they sought mainland mates. Rachel's fantasy followed the story — the will dictating that the twins must seek partners and marry within two years, as a condition of keeping this island they loved.

But Larry and Beryl!?

Rachel could not match up the pairs. It could only have happened as a business arrangement. Neither of the couples appeared to have children, so perhaps the marriages were never consummated … but she baulked at the associated images.

Physical aspects aside, they could not have been so island-sheltered that they didn't realise how destructive it would be to live with someone you despised, even with separate bedrooms. Rachel thought of her ill-matched parents, boasting now of their 50 years of marriage. No endurance marathon for her, she re-affirmed grimly.

Maybe the prawning season makes up for the rest of the year: Charles over here with Elizabeth, Larry on the loose up north and perhaps even Beryl finding the energy to paint more than her nails red in Rocky – but Rachel did not convince herself.

A dip might clear her head. She let herself drift gently over the slight swells, the rhythm as soothing as the rocking of a cradle. Reluctantly she turned over and began breaststroking back in, idly scanning the cliffs, lower on this side. It wasn't sunset yet; she'd have time to meet Jo at the jetty.

Then she saw it – coming round the bend from where the house must be; a white figure this time. Rachel hurried to shore. Grabbing her towel, she stumbled up the shingle. It was a person, Rachel was sure now, but of what sort she could not make out. But she would; she must catch up. Clawing her way over rocks and tussocks, she climbed to the clifftop, thankful she'd kept her sandshoes on. She reached the glitter of the headland path, head throbbing, legs shaky.

The path ahead was empty. She began to run, but underestimated her weakness, and fell, savagely grazing her knees on the sharp shellgrit. Hobbling to sit on a fallen paperbark trunk, she snuffled back tears of frustration and pain. She allowed herself a half-bitten howl of exasperation, eyes tightly closed as if to will it all unhappened.

A slight crunch of shellgrit and a whiff of lavender quickly opened her eyes to a white handkerchief, lace-edged, being dangled in front of her nose by a white-gloved hand.

"Allow me," said a voice, as thin and English as the finest china tea cup. Rachel's blurry eyes flicked from the hand up a long white sleeve to a high neckline; a sagging and crepey face, heavily and palely powdered, somehow unutterably sad despite the eyes being hidden behind dark sunglasses; pale, almost white hair, stiffly curled, the whole shaded by a large befrilled white parasol, its carved cane handle held tightly in the other glove.

"Thank you," managed Rachel as she took the handkerchief. The vision nodded slightly and glided on, a hazy white shape on the white path, long skirts ballooning behind it in the breeze.

She tried to tell Jo about it in between gasps as she bathed her poor knees, self-inflicting the necessary agony of teasing out shellgrit fragments. "It wasn't really an old-fashioned dress, just long. But white gloves!?"

Were it not for the handkerchief soaking in a bowl, Jo would have suggested sunstruck hallucination, an extension of Rachel's imagination. As she hung the thin fabric up to dry, she noted the embroidered initials in one corner: E.A.

"Do you think your ghost could be Mr. A's sister? Larry's wife?"

"Oh no!" cried Rachel, wincing. "She couldn't possibly be ..." but knew there could be no other explanation on this small island.

As if on cue, they heard Larry's jeep pull up outside.

He appeared in the doorway with a bottle of Dettol. "Heard one a yers had a bit uv a spill. The missus thought ya might need some a this."

Taking it, Jo asked him to thank his wife. "Does she go for a walk every evening? Rach thought she'd seen her up there before."

"Yeah, well, she can't take any sunlight, see, bein' one a them whiteys ... and a bloody nuisance that is up 'ere, I tell ya! ... so she always goes then to get outta the house, get a bitta exercise."

"Well, tell her we'll return her handkerchief when it's dry: so E.A. stands for …?"

"Ah, that'd be an old one. Elizabeth Armstrong, see? I call 'er Lizzie meself, but 'er family useta go the whole hog. Chuckie still does."

That night, Rachel drank a great deal of rum for the pain. She awoke in a sweat from a nightmare, where a strange caged white creature, like an albino lemur, its huge sad eyes fixed on hers in mute appeal, paced around and around the inside of its cage, its long tail dragging behind it, while outside, hairy apes slavered and grunted and rattled the bars.

Stumbling to the sink for water, she saw the handkerchief pegged beside the tea towel. Her hand seized it just as Jo called, "Rach, what are you doing? I'll get you some water; come and lie back down, you idiot!"

"I think we should get you to a doctor, Rach. You must have quite an infection; you're very hot. Larry says we can go back on the mail boat today, OK?"

Rachel nodded, too remote in her fever to argue. It was not until Jo woke her up later that she realised that everything was packed.

"But aren't we coming back? We've still a few days to go …"

"What's the point? You won't be doing anything with those knees; you can hardly stand up! Now come on, Rach, here's the jeep to give us a lift to the jetty."

"But …" demurred Rachel weakly; there was a bigger "but", only she couldn't think what it was.

When she glimpsed Charles Armstrong at the wheel of the Shady Lady as it passed the mail boat, she remembered briefly. Her hand went to her pocket, scrunching the thin handkerchief. Elizabeth … I'll write … I'll help … somehow …

But, safely back in her southern city, her knees healed, the vividness of her sympathy dimmed, the tropical drama diminished — she didn't get around to it.

Yet she kept the handkerchief, ever intending to. Every so often her eye would come upon it, neatly folded at the back of a drawer, waiting in mute reproach.

Then, through the safety of the solid world that her always practical partners created for her, suddenly there would burst forth the swish of sea on pebbles, the salty circling of unanswered questions … and the gritty guilt of the unanswered appeal.

Oh Rachel, you and your imagination …

RUAIRI MURPHY is a librarian and writer living in Hobart. He is the author of Two sets of books, *an award-winning collection of stories about the lives of fictional Hobart Library staff.*

The collared leopard

RUAIRI MURPHY

My father's advice on marriage was uncomplicated: let no woman put a leash around your neck. He would rest his hand on my shoulder and whisper this to me as my mother screamed at him from an adjacent room. Then he would pour himself another glass of whisky, a generous measure in a steady stream that put him in the ground before my twelfth birthday. But in November 1929, seventeen years after his death and on the eve of my marriage to a ship merchant's daughter, I met my father again. He was standing behind me in Hobart's Beaumaris Zoo as we watched a leopard surrender the last of his dignity in a woman's arms.

Back then I worked for Prestige Limited, a national hosiery and knitwear manufacturer that specialised in fine silken stockings. The textile industry had boomed after the war but by late 1929 the Depression had begun its precipitous decline and I was ordered to travel from Melbourne to Hobart to lay off employees at the local mill. I took no pleasure in this duty but I was excited about the visit.

Company etiquette held that all guests were to be afforded a field trip and I was confident that I might persuade my host to allow me an afternoon to summit Mount Wellington, whose basalt columns I greatly admired. My host, the Mill's manager, would sooner have run me through one of his gear-toothed machines than extend any kind of courtesy, but he was a company man, all of whom can unfailingly be relied upon to discharge their duty.

When he proposed a tour of the local zoo, I politely declined, citing a trip to Southern Rhodesia two years earlier where I had hunted much of the big game that makes menageries attractive to people. I had barely begun to voice my alternative plan when he interrupted to remind me that etiquette in business applies equally to both parties, and furthermore any deviation from that principle might easily lead me to join the men I sent to the breadline. His precise words were far coarser than these and he took great relish in delivering them, safe in the knowledge that I, too, was a company man. My deference was grudging but swift. By that afternoon I was on a tram bound for Beaumaris Zoo.

My abominable mood at being so roundly defeated by this man was slightly tapered when I was met at the zoo's entrance by a tall, broad-shouldered woman with short hair, worn in the finger-wave style that was popular among fashionable ladies at the time. She introduced herself as Alison Reid and was the daughter of the zoo's curator. She explained that the zoo was closed for the day and that we had the place to ourselves.

I liked her immediately. Her tone was soft and her gaze unassuming. It was a pleasant change from Betty, my fiancée, whom I'd quarrelled with when departing Melbourne. We'd been introduced only the year before and widely considered a good match. But cracks had begun appearing in our relationship, none so large as when I went away. On this latest occasion, after handing over my pay cheque to her, she had refused to give me my full allowance, convinced that I would spend it on beer and fast women. I thought of the ring I had placed on Betty's finger and it drew my gaze to Alison's hand. I was pleased to see that she wore no ring.

"It's a beautiful afternoon," Alison said. "Would you care to take a stroll through the grounds?"

Alison was careful here to use an upward inflection on the word "stroll". This was a sign of good breeding and a rare courtesy extended to fighting men beyond a certain age. I told her that I had indeed been injured in the war, but by a bullet through the neck, which temporarily paralysed my larynx and meant only that I had to shut up for a few weeks. The incident was, of course, far graver than this, entailing months of despair and loneliness in a foreign hospital and a bout of near-fatal pneumonia. But one quickly learns to make light of tragedy if one hopes ever to return to polite society. Alison was alive to my deliberate depreciation and betrayed nothing. She dutifully laughed and, our hands clasped behind our backs, we began our clockwise journey through the gardens.

Beaumaris Zoo exhibited nothing to counter my initial prejudice toward it. It was like all zoos. It smelled of damp straw and spoiled apples. The enclosures were cracked concrete walls or rusted iron cages. And the animals were unexceptional. They either lay sprawled and sullen upon the ground, or else mindlessly paced a single side of their boundary. On occasion one would bark or cry out and be answered by another, but otherwise Alison and I roamed about them undisturbed.

She spoke about the Zoo's history and the animals her father had acquired since its opening. I recall now only one of these stories, about a pair of sun bears who a few years earlier had escaped from their enclosure and later had been shot and killed by police. I recall the story for no other reason than that Alison became upset during its telling.

Notwithstanding my choice of fiancée, I have always found compassion in a woman to be an irresistible quality. It lends itself to forgive weakness and impulse in all creatures, and when we paused on a wooden bridge that overlooked a duck pond, I placed my hand in the small of Alison's back.

The afternoon up until that point had had an air of inevitability about it. Had Alison herself not set the tone with her explicit declaration that we had the zoo to ourselves? As far as I was concerned, we were two adults enjoying one another's intellect and gliding inexorably toward intimacy. She might playfully resist me at first, as is the female want, but we would soon end up in each other's arms, ideally on a bed of soft and sweet-smelling hay in some hospitable garden shed. Later, I would have the additional pleasure of recounting to the Mill's manager that never was a finer time had by man or beast in a zoo.

Needless to say the afternoon took a markedly different turn. No sooner did my hand alight upon Alison's delicate curvature than she slipped from my hold with a speed and deftness that would have rivalled the goldfish that swam in the murky water beneath us. Her laugh, having so recently enjoyed a knowing, carefree quality, at once became forced and shrill. Hurrying away from me, she transformed into a silly girl, one who bounced on the balls of her feet like Dorothy on her way through Oz. She called back, "Would you like to meet my greatest chum in the Zoo?"

Any sense of propriety I retained to that point promptly vanished. I saw the banality of the rest of the afternoon unfolding before me and I detested it. I had spent enough time in this wretched place to honour my obligation. I thought briefly of feigning illness, before deciding instead I would request a phone to contact the Telegraph Office and then quietly slip away. This excuse had the advantage of possessing a kernel of truth, as I had promised to send Betty at least two telegrams per day while I was away.

Before I could catch up with Alison, she entered a small white building atop a rise in the grounds. I followed her inside, then froze. There were two cages in the room, one either side of me, separated by a narrow corridor. In each of these cages was a leopard. In the cage on my left was Alison. She was kneeling before one of the leopards, tapping the nails of her left hand on the wooden floorboards. Intermittently, she whispered, "Mike."

When Alison looked across at me, she smiled and patted the air in front of her. I took a backward step and crouched. I saw then that in her right hand she held a chain. It sparkled in the afternoon sunlight that shone through a small window at the top of the cage. Alison made no attempt to hide the chain from the leopard, but rather held it out, like a proposal.

For its part, the leopard appeared uninterested in Alison. It sat sphinx-like, staring and slow-blinking at a corner of the cage. It was watching her, though. I had no doubt it was watching me, too.

This stand-off lasted perhaps a minute, during which Alison edged forward on one knee toward the leopard. I became conscious that my breathing was rigid and shallow. When she was close enough, she placed the chain around the animal's neck and tightened the collar. Then, slowly, she rose to her feet, the leopard following like a marionette. I stood and pressed my whole body against the cage as they passed.

"He's as gentle as a lamb," Alison said when we were outside the building. "I can put my hand in his mouth and he never bites."

I didn't doubt her claims, but I thought it best that Mike remain on the opposite side of her to me as we continued our walk. The afternoon had taken another unexpected turn from our episode on the bridge and my plans to flee were all but forgotten. When we had travelled perhaps fifty meters without incident, I inquired how she had tamed the animal.

"Mike's mother had twins," Alison said, "and the nasty old thing actually ate one of them. So I just had to take charge of the other little fellow to save his life." She looked down affectionately at the leopard who kept perfect pace with her. "We had a job to get him to take any nourishment at all, but eventually got him accustomed to sucking a bottle of milk, and fed him just like a baby for six months." She reached down and smoothed the fur on Mike's back. "He is a fine chap now. Aren't you, Mike?"

Mike gave no answer. He was slinking along, his body and tail low to the ground and his head bowed. His eyes glanced anxiously about him. He seemed not to notice Alison's touch, nor her repeatedly calling his name in an effort to get him to look up at her. Indeed, he gave every appearance of one who does not wish to be seen.

I was suddenly mindful of how the other animals must have viewed him. Here was a predator that, with the possible exception of the lions, the elephants, and the polar bears, had the breeding to tear the life from their bodies and the flesh from their bones. In spite of his impressive size, he was light and graceful on his feet. If all that were not enough, he was also bound in the most magnificent coat, as striking as any bird of paradise.

Yet here he was being walked like a dog. I looked for the first time with interest into the decrepit enclosures that lined our path. Would the animals inside them leap up from their listlessness to look and laugh at this chastened creature? Or would they simply turn away in disgust, unable to bare such an undignified parade? My right hand rose up of its own accord and loosened the knot on my tie. It was Betty's favourite, the one she insisted I wear on all our outings together.

Opposite the spider monkeys' cage, we came upon a wooden bench, and Alison, looking pale, asked that we sit. I assumed that she was once more distressed by an animal's fate. We had just passed the enclosure that held the Tasmanian tiger, an endemic marsupial similar to a hyena but with a kangaroo's hindquarters and tiger stripes on its back. This specimen clearly disagreed with captivity. Its body was appallingly thin and its coat was frayed to the point of exposing skin. Like many of the other animals it ceaselessly trod its boundary, but there was a pitiful urgency about this one's desire for escape, a frantic to-and-fro scurry that wore a track into the dirt floor. I have since learned that this creature, now dead, was likely the last of its kind, a plight that must have weighed heavily upon the curator's daughter. Alison's compassion resurfaced again, and I saw my opportunity to try to resurrect the afternoon to its initial promise.

I sat close to Alison and told her that Prestige would shortly be diversifying into lingerie. This was patently untrue, but I enjoyed the effect this word had on women. They either assumed that you were about to ask them if they wore such garments, or else that you were the sort of man for whom seeing ladies in their underwear was an everyday occurrence. One or the other was fine. Both was preferable.

Alison contemplated neither. Or if she did, such thoughts were immediately extinguished by whatever puritanical force ruled her. Once more she effortlessly slid away from me and fled toward her greatest chum, her finest chap.

"Isn't he handsome?" she said of Mike.

I'd forgotten all about the leopard, such was his meekness. Mike sat obediently at her feet. His head was turned away from us, and I followed his gaze to the white building from which we had all come.

Reading my mind, Alison said, "He doesn't like to be taken out of his cage. He is always anxious to get back." She absently twisted and untwisted Mike's chain around her wrist. "That, to my way of thinking, rather disposes of the idea held by some people that animals in cages must be unhappy."

With that inane comment, Alison bent down and fed her arms underneath Mike's ribcage. I saw what she intended and briefly considered stopping her. It's one thing to lead an animal on a leash, quite another to treat it like a stuffed toy. But Mike was limp in her arms, and with an exaggerated grunt Alison lifted his upper body and positioned it on her lap. Mike's paws now dangled before him, and his ears flattened under the weight of her emphatic strokes. His humiliation was complete.

As if by way of apology, Mike finally looked up at me, raising only his eyes.

That was the moment I felt my father standing behind me. He was not shouting, nor did he smell of whiskey. It was my mid-morning father, revived and steady. It was the man who most closely resembled stories of his youth, told to me years after his death by aunts and uncles whom I'd never known existed. The man who raced in a 1908 model Motobloc at Sandown when it was nothing more than a dirt track. The man who went fifteen rounds with Reginald "Snowy" Baker while boxing for Melbourne University. The "plenty rugged" man in faded photographs who stood straight and tall in tailored suits, a proud posture I sometimes glimpsed during the periods my mother went away.

I knew that man's touch, and I knew it again as he rested his hand upon my shoulder and gave it a gentle squeeze. That touch served a single purpose, to remind me that the world was as he said it was, and if I didn't believe him, then I should just take a look at what was right in front of me.

I didn't turn to confirm he was standing there. I didn't need to. Mike was staring right at him.

I hastily stood and removed my wallet from my coat pocket. From my wallet I removed a sixpence, which was the admission price to the Zoo, and laid it on the bench next to Alison and Mike.

"For the animals," I told her. Then I thanked her for the tour and said that I must leave at once.

I was pleased to see Alison's decorum momentarily fail her. She smiled openly in relief at the news of my departure before quickly recovering herself. She looked down at Mike and stroked him as she spoke. "You have another engagement?"

"Quite the contrary," I said, turning to leave. "I need to go and break one."

Born in Canada, JASON SPONGBERG moved to Tasmania in 2002 and later became an Australian citizen. He has been shortlisted for the Australian/Vogel Award and was a quarter finalist in the Amazon Breakthrough Novel Contest. He teaches English as an Additional Language to migrants and former refugees.

Screen funeral

JASON SPONGBERG

Terry Bowles didn't understand what was happening with his computer, but then again he rarely did — not because he was dumb, but because he'd allowed himself to fall behind, which was something he'd promised himself he'd never do. He was sitting in front of his laptop at the kitchen table, coffee in hand, chicken soup bubbling on the stove. He was wearing his black suit with a white shirt and blue tie. He'd had everything dry-cleaned. Even his shoes were shiny. He'd nicked himself shaving again, but it was a small cut and he didn't think anyone would notice. At the age of 72, Terry had come to accept that certain things were beyond his control.

"Come on, come on," he muttered. He kept his voice low so as not to wake up his wife, Ellen. She had dementia and he wished — guiltily — that she would sleep more. Sometimes she knew him and sometimes she didn't, but he had to wait all day for thirty seconds of normalcy. The rest was difficult.

Why can't I see anything? Following instructions was his strong suit. He'd been in the army, after all, fifty years earlier. Then a teacher. He knew *all* about instructions. Open the email, click on the blue letters. The 'link.' But then everything had gone haywire. He put on his headphones but there was no sound. The screen still showed just the email from the funeral home in Canada and nothing else. Checking his watch, he realized he had only four minutes before his brother's funeral was about to begin.

"Hello?" he said into the microphone. "Can anyone hear me? Do you copy?" He briefly considered tapping on the thing in Morse code, but that was silly. Nobody understood that anymore. He'd been a radio operator in Vietnam. Carrying around a backpack had made him a massive target. Now what was he? Just another old bastard in a retirement village. Here he was in Australia during a pandemic, and his little brother had gone and married some Canadian woman forty-odd years ago, why had he done that? Because she was beautiful. And dead too, now. Who wasn't dead?

Me and Ellen aren't dead. My sister's not dead. My kids aren't dead, neither are the grandkids. Old Poppy Terry's still here, playing golf and walking the latest dog in a long line of dead dogs. Terry glanced down at Frank, his black-but-greying poodle. He was pushing thirteen now, old in dog years, but still happy. Still going. Was that the point now? To keep going beyond all hope of hope?

"Shit," Terry whispered. He took off the headphones and placed them gently on the table. He straightened his tie. He found his phone after several minutes of wandering around the kitchen – quietly, always quietly, because Ellen listened in her bloody sleep – and stepped outside the front door to ring his son. He put on his mask. It was a blindingly bright summer's day. Sprinklers were feeding lawns, but that wouldn't continue for long once they tightened up the water restrictions. It was going to be a scorcher of a summer, he could feel it in his bones.

His son's number went straight to voicemail. Damn.

Sneaking back inside, Terry removed his mask again and confronted the laptop. His son had said something about the TV being connected to the Internet. Maybe the funeral was on there? He turned on the large flatscreen in the lounge room – carefully, so carefully muting it the second it sparked to life – and cycled through the channels and streaming services. No funeral. Shows about fishing, shows about cooking, some program about a guy with twenty girlfriends, but no funeral. So how was the TV connected to the Internet, or his laptop? It made no sense. His phone had the Internet as well, but there was no funeral on the screen. His email app just showed the same blue letters as his laptop, just on a much smaller screen that required him to stretch his bifocals to their limits.

The funeral was starting. Four minutes *late* now.

There was a speaker his son had bought him – you spoke into it and it played music. But he didn't think that would work. He wasn't an idiot, for God's sake! His heart began to pound in his ears. His hands were sweaty. The irises his daughter-in-law had brought over a few days previously were drooping in their water; the chicken soup was boiling now, well and truly done, so he turned the burner off. The soup always calmed his wife down if she woke up from her nap. Something about it maybe reminded her of the old days in their tiny apartment in Molle Street, ants crawling up the walls, shower that barely drained, no computers, no mobiles, just newspapers and each other and songs on the radio.

My son's going to think I'm a fool. And everyone at the funeral will think I couldn't be bothered showing up even online. They changed the time for me. Eighteen hours ahead here in Oz, they changed the time for me so I wouldn't have to get up early. Eighteen hours ... did he have the day wrong? No, he'd accounted for that. It was the 24th here but the 23rd there, and the funeral was definitely on the 23rd. Picking up his phone again, he went into contacts and brought up his sister's mobile number. There was supposed to be some cheap way of calling her — some other app — but numbers made sense. Double-zero double-one, then another one for the country code, then the area code and phone number, easy-peasy.

She didn't answer. Just like when he rang his son, it went straight to voicemail. She probably had her phone on silent during the funeral like a responsible person. He went back to his laptop. FUNERAL FOR KEITH BOWLES. That was right. It didn't say how his brother had died of a heart attack at the young age of 69, but the name was right, the town was right, everything was right, why didn't it work?

Terry tightened his hands into fists. How long had it been since he'd spoken to Keith? Six months? And the last words hadn't been *I love you* or something, it had been *see ya mate*. He thought of his brother, five years old, running on the beach and yelling about sharks, he'd always tried to convince his older sister there were sharks everywhere because he loved it when a girl was scared, when she squealed. Terry stared at the laptop screen and shuddered. Tears gathered in his eyes but didn't leave them. Don't think ill of the dead, sure, but Keith hadn't been a very nice guy sometimes, when you got down to brass tacks. Nice guy or not, the eulogy was nice and had taken two weeks to write. He wondered if anyone else was sitting there in the funeral home, or if anyone else was having trouble connecting online.

Ten more minutes passed. Terry clicked on everything he could. No use. He Googled the funeral on his phone, to no avail. He grew louder and louder, swearing, grinding his teeth, until he heard the telltale sound of his wife turning over in bed and getting up. It was only a two-bedroom unit. Sound carried.

Ellen walked into the room tying her pink bathrobe. Her eyes were strangely focused. "Did you click on the blue writing?"

"Yes. Of course."

"Let me try."

She moved her hand over the mouse. "This isn't plugged in." She found the USB connector and plugged it into the side of the laptop. "There you go. Now click on it."

Terry stared at her. There was no time. He had to click on it. When he did, the screen came to life and he could see his sister talking. He hoped she could see him, but he didn't think she could. *Why in the hell did Ellen know that and I didn't? Plug in the mouse!* But now Ellen was heading for the chicken soup, and the last thing he wanted was for her to dump it all over herself and get hurt. She was muttering something now: "Three of them in there, three, didn't have their seatbelts on, going to crash and who are you again? Who are you?" She confronted her husband as she always did. "What are *you* doing in here? I'll call the police!"

"Ellen, it's me. I'm watching a funeral."

"Excuses, excuses," she said. Terry got her a bowl of soup, sat her down at the table, and watched her. He could watch his wife and the funeral at the same time if he paid enough attention. Just like juggling. Just keep the balls in the air, don't drop one, not a single mistake. Ellen stared off into the distance, her soup forgotten, but she looked happy in an odd way, like she was seeing something he wasn't. She looked beautiful with the sun lighting up her hair like that.

My brother's dead.

Terry put on his headphones and watched the rest of the funeral. The soup in front of his wife steamed a little, then gradually went cold.

ROMY TARA WENZEL is a writer and artist on Melukerdee country, Tasmania, exploring mythology and ecology from an animist perspective. Her preoccupation is with liminal states: the spaces between becoming and unbecoming, wildness and refuge, inter-species communication and ecstatic transformation. Publications this year include short stories in Dark Mountain, Cunning Folk, and Folklore for Resistance, amongst others. Her novel Heartwood was shortlisted for the 2021 Speculate Prize. Instagram @the_quiet_wilds

The unbecoming

ROMY TARA WENZEL

The beast was at her back door, trapping her inside the house.

This wasn't the first time. Last week it arrived with a jellyfish in its mouth, leaving the ghostly thing at her doorstep like a cat bringing a dead bird home. *I am the sea*, it said with its midnight eyes, and Fenn drew back to the safety of the porch and the climbing roses that asked nothing of her except a light Spring pruning. Who knew what this creature wanted; she didn't speak Sea.

Ocean levels were rising. Fenn had known the sea would creep into her backyard one day, but she hadn't expected it to *walk* in on flippers like flint knives, as long as Fenn's arms. Sides segmented like an orange, black and mottled with stars, throat flaccid in that obscene, prehistoric way. Why was it here? *Climate change*, Fenn thought with dull rage. Wildlife had rebelled against it in more concrete ways than humans had. Whales had changed their migration patterns.

Bioluminescent algae were lighting up the coast like a Christmas tree. A hundred thousand salmon escaped a battery fish farm last week. That last was human stupidity, not climate change, but Fenn preferred to think of it as an act of salmon resistance. She had slipped her net too, two years ago.

When the divorce was finalised, she'd arrived on Bruny with a suitcase and half a house in cash. Enough to buy a beachside shack. There were a few downsides; the wind stripped the weatherboards, sea air got into everything and swelled it with salt and lichen. The water pipes had rusted and Fenn had to collect her drinking water from the tank outside, which froze over on cold nights. The front door seized in place her first winter, and the windows didn't close properly, letting in the mosquitoes. She filled the gaps with expanding foam, and it billowed out into clouds of unsightly yellow mushrooms. With no openings to the outside world except for the back door, she was stuck in the house.

Fenn sighed. Little things got to her these days, and only little things remedied them. If only she could have a cup of tea, she'd figure out this monster in the backyard. A nice, soothing cup of tea, and she'd know what to do. *Scotland*, the tea towel curtain announced in blue and white, as she let it fall. Scotland was her motherland, but she had a collection of tea towels with island maps. *I should have hung the tea towel of England in the window; England was always better against invaders. Too late now. Everything is too late now.*

Fenn checked the kettle. Water swished around the heating coils; not enough for a new brew. She pulled the curtain back. The beast was a dark knoll on the sandy lawn. Beyond him, the water tank, and beyond that, the ocean. The Bruny Five were at the shoreline, rubbing their arms and legs, pulling on their swim caps, not a wetsuit in sight. They waved at her over the fence, buoyant with anticipation. The Bruny Five never missed a day. Crones all, more advanced in years than she was, but youth in their faces, their scrawny muscles, and the clarity of their gaze. Fenn watched with horror as, one by one, they disappeared into the sea, that gobbled up whole ships and would have no qualms taking down a few scrawny old ladies. In her mind, Fenn saw them snatched by a shark, an orca, pierced by a ray, swallowed by a whale. *I'd be right, at least,* she thought with glee. *I would be right about something.*

She picked up the morning cup she'd left on the windowsill, swirled the dregs and peered at the leaves in the bottom. A half circle, a mast, and a sail. Wasn't it always a boat? Her grandmother had said people always saw what they most feared in their futures. More often than not, their fears came to pass. Fenn took a swig, made a face, and spat it back. Cold as a witch's tit, as her Granny used to say. Damn and blast, she needed tea. Could she knock out the foam, squeeze through a window and walk down to the general store? If she hauled her old bones through one without guillotining herself, she'd never get it closed again. She could not get out. She could not get out.

She felt the anxiety rising inside her like an incoming tide. The air temperature shifted, a thick, cold front. *Not now. Keep calm.* Deep breath. *Count to four. Hold. To four. Exhale two, three, four. Carry on.* Her divorce lawyer taught her that one, but she'd always felt those tides of anxiety inside her. They were stronger, now that she was officially menopausal. She wriggled her toes into the cocoon of her Hush Puppy slippers. After two decades of nursing clogs, she wore the Puppies round the clock. No one else was around to judge anymore. Skin and fleece, a marriage that she was on board with, a tradition that ran through her ancestral line. *There you are. Contained. Safe.* And with safety, came the rage.

The world was fucked. Even in Tasmania, where seasons layered within seasons like an onion and sometimes you found Spring inside of Autumn or Winter inside of Spring. The fishers and divers knew it, Antarctic expeditions knew it, the Bruny Five knew it, wombats knew it, whales knew it. Even Fenn, who preferred to live without a television or mobile phone — *why the fuck would I invite in more drama, when I just spent two years divorcing it* — knew it. She saw the plagues of sea lice on the shore, smelled the red and ash air of fire season. Maimed seals, sea pollution, weather events. And now, this black-eyed, leather-bound creature in her yard that she watched from behind a map of Scotland.

She picked up the phone.

"Olive," she said into the cream mouthpiece, and paused, realising the ludicrousness of the situation. But this was her daughter, not her ex-husband. Her daughter would understand. She spiralled the cord around her finger. "A turtle is outside. Right outside, at my door. Long as I am, and twice as round. And I've put on weight since I saw you last," she added, to explain how serious it was.

"Ooh," Olive crooned. "A leatherback! She should be further north, this time of year."

"She?" Fenn looked doubtfully at the hulking creature outside. "It's a dinosaur, Olive. Gotta be a male."

"Males don't leave the ocean. Leatherbacks get big. Real big."

"It's holding me hostage. I can't get to the tank to make a cup of tea."

Olive laughed. "She won't chase you down, Mum. Probably injured, to be out of the water. Report it to wildlife rescue, then go fill the kettle. To her, you're just another animal."

Fenn hung up the phone. Olive was practical about these things. But the truth was, it was Olive who had consolidated Fenn's fear of the sea when she chose marine science as her major. A small daughter, disappearing into a vast sea. The ocean was hungry, and big enough to eat the world, if it wanted to. Likely one day it would. She glanced at the dark shape through the transparent curtain. *One bite at a time.*

Fenn unfolded her dusty laptop and filled out the form to report injured wildlife. She opened another tab and her ring finger stroked the S key. She'd seen plenty of misinformation in the doctor's office obtained through Dr Google. But she wanted to be ready. She had to assess her risks.

Do turtles bite? she typed. With bone-shattering force, Google replied. Fenn wrinkled her brow. Turtles didn't have teeth, she'd seen it with her own eyes, when Olive was a kid. Olive had laughed – that same, tinkling laugh that she had now – at the zoo tortoise with the gummy, toothless smile. Dr Google was a liar. But she tried a Google Image search just to be sure.

Farrk, she swore in a soft Scottish purr. Turtles didn't have teeth in their *mouths*. They had a cavern of teeth all the way down their throat, a bramble turned inside out, a tangle of one-way thorns made for catching and shredding. That monster snapped at your hand, you'd never get your finger out again. She'd pulled enough fish hooks out at the nursing station to know that she didn't want to risk a few dozen fish hooks with a few hundred kilos attached to them.

I could make a run for it. How fast could turtles run, anyway? 35 kilometres per hour, Google replied. Pretty fast for an animal that can weigh up to 900 kilos. *Google is laughing at me*, Fenn thought in despair. The anxiety rose, her heart fluttered in her chest. The air temperature shifted, a thick, cold front. The walls, the walls were wet. Darkening with the damp. Blue and black swelled her feet, her mouth, her eyes. She widened her lips, and the sea tumbled out.

No, no, no. She sucked it back in. Deep breath. *Count to four. Hold. To four. Exhale the water back into the sea, two, three, four.*

She checked outside, to reassure herself it hadn't come any closer. In a nightmare, every time she checked, it would be a little closer, until she'd turn around and it would be in the room with her. But the leatherback was still in the same place, a big rock on the lawn. Over the fence the Bruny Five were finishing up, glistening bodies slipping from the water as if they were sea. They moved differently after a swim, transformed from elderly swimmers to creatures finned and scaled, the light catching at their wet bodies, diffusing wrinkles and shimmering skin. All the friendly greetings were gone from them; they were animals of the deep, black-eyed and emptied of conversation. They smiled back at you if you said hello, but the smiles were rabid, animals bearing fangs.

Fenn opened a new tab. National Geographic would tell her, National Geographic wouldn't lie. She soothed her rapid heartbeat with holiday blue waters, sweet hatchlings in hands, and fun facts. Leatherback spines were not teeth but papillae, a gentle word that made Fenn think of butterflies. Like so many others, they were endangered because of human-wrought destruction. Only one in a thousand reached adulthood. One in a *thousand*. Fenn had lost five of six babies. As a nurse she'd seen others lose more, but one in a thousand was plain unfair.

She squinted at the leatherback on her lawn. Likely a mother at some point, like her. The night eyes stared back, unblinking. *Wait! What was that?* Fenn blinked, pushed her glasses up her nose. *Surely not.* But there it was, another one; a glinting tear, slipping from the black eye, trickling down the wrinkled cheek.

Fenn picked up the phone.

"Olive." Fenn paused. "The turtle is crying."

Olive laughed. "Adorable, Mum. But they excrete sea salt via their eyes. Salt glands."

Fenn kept silent. She knew that it wasn't adorable, and it wasn't because of salt glands that the turtle was crying. The turtle was crying because of her babies. But Olive was a scientist and scientists were sticklers for facts, even when there was a better story. A story that made the monster less monstrous.

"Well, I just wanted to check. I better rustle up some dinner. The Bruny Five are out of the water, and that means it's getting late."

"Wouldn't hurt you to get out there with them, Mum. You know what my naturopath says? Treat the sickness with a small dose of the poison. I've heard of folks taking a little sea water by mouth, even. The least you can do is get in the water. Why live on an island if you don't get in the ocean?"

Why, indeed. *Because I am looking for edges*, Fenn could have responded. *Because I myself am an island, and my tides are rising, and I have to find the edges in things or I will disappear.*

. . .

She woke up at the window, her head collapsed onto her shoulder. Her neck writhed back into position. *Bloody old bones. Bloody collapsing neck.* The tea towel shone with dusk light. The moon was up, a long moon like a cuttlefish, stretched along the blushing sunset reflected on the tank. Purple shadows fell long across the grass, and the black lump had turned midnight blue and flattened into the sand. It had gone. The edges of everything blurred, like the world was draped in dark silk. Perhaps that was just her cataracts.

She wondered if turtles got cataracts, and what the sea looked like then. *Like looking from inside a jellyfish*, she speculated. That would be an ironic development, for a turtle. Their version of Jonah, she supposed, if turtles were to pen a Bible, with gull quills and squid ink, and little slippered flippers. *You're getting silly*, she told herself. *Silly and old.* She made her mouth a thin line. That was why she left her husband, after all. For the freedom to be silly.

She opened the screen door and scanned the yard. The night itself felt like the leatherback, watching with its black eyes. Was it behind the gate, waiting to attack? Perhaps it was listening for movement inside the house. Did turtles have good hearing? She assessed the gravel path and thought about the crunch the Hush Puppies made when she walked to the car.

Barefoot, she must go barefoot.

Fenn slid off one slipper and left it on the porch. Her foot looked cold and white, blue mycelium running under the skin. A wrinkled, ugly old thing. *Old, joyously old, fine wine and standing stones and druid oaks old,* she reminded herself. *Crone old.* Her toes wiggled in the other slipper for one last moment of comfort, and then she slid that off too. The gravel was vibrant, sharp on her soles. *I'm bleeding,* Fenn thought, but steeled her Highlander blood and took another step. *I have not bled for many moons, I can afford a little blood.*

She reached the tank, and leaned down to twist the tap. Something moved in the corner of her eye. She froze and turned to face the monster.

This creature was not a hulking mountain of spine-throated turtle, but made of many tiny parts. The sand seethed with tiny limbs breaking open sand, fumbling in all directions, black teardrops breaking apart, coming together again. *A hatchling.* The terror dropped away. These were not monsters at her back door, these were the hatchlings that fit in your palm. *One in a thousand. Life is so short.*

The hatchlings propelled themselves across the grass, under a thousand winking stars. They dipped their flippers with sand, flipped it over their soft shells. Fenn followed them, bleeding on the sand. The waves roared and their flippers sped up, as if the roaring of the waves was a sweet mother song calling them in. And Fenn's bare feet followed them down to the water. The turtles nosed their way in, and one by one, disappeared under the black ink of the waves.

The sky and the sea had no horizon, but smudged into a single black entity. The wind tossed her grey hair. All the water at her feet reminded her she still had not had her cup of tea. But what did fish drink? And whales? Penguins on long sea voyages? Leatherbacks?

Thirsty, so thirsty. She did not feel like she could make it all the way back to the tank.

The water came to her first, stretching its edges to slip between her toes. *Not so bad*, she thought, as the sea slipped away again, coy. She leaned down to the water, touched her lips to it as if she would kiss the cold salt body, made her tongue into a spoon, drank headily of the salt, the shadows, the kelp strands, the seahorse eggs, the sea-lice, the baby jellyfish, took it all inside herself. Welcomed it in.

Afterwards, her body purged the water onto the sand. Fenn felt a great emptying. *Two, three, four.* As if all the things she had pushed down over the years were coming up, as if the water was combing the walls of her insides for any secrets she might have lodged into the archives of her organ walls. The salt lingered on her tongue as if it were bound to it. The salt would remain. *Exhale, two, three, four.*

Fenn sat on the sandbank, half-wet, the in-between where her body met the land and the sea dropped off into the expanse. She rubbed the sand over her body, draped herself in seaweed, and looked out to the faultless horizon. She let the waves lap at her belly and pool in her navel, let the sea sing over her. It had more songs than she could count, *two, three, four, five, six, seven* … now that she listened the sea was not full of threats and violence, but a melody utterly indifferent to the human ear. *Just another animal.* The wind furrowed the water's edge into patterns that she recognised in her own aging skin, spotted and wrinkled. Drew back again, revealing the parts of the island that were hidden underwater, shifted the boundaries of the sea and of the island, too. Off in the distance, waves being born, whales singing.